"You may not like me, Mr. Austin," she said, returning to their earlier formality, "but we're very similar, you and I. We put our patients first. We put in the hours. Perhaps because neither of us has anything else in our life..."

Her harsh words hung in the stiff silence. The tense seconds in the wake of her outrageously rude accusations made Darcy's breath come in incensed pants. He, too, was breathing hard, his dark eyes locked with her blue ones.

Had she flushed her career down the drain?

And yet a current of suspense hung in the air, tendrils of energy snaking between them, sparks of heat and fire.

Darcy's indignation became swamped by the absurd urge to kiss Joe's arrogant, sculpted mouth.

No! Madness.

Except he seemed to sense her wildly inappropriate thoughts. His gaze dropped to her lips. He inhaled sharply. His eyes landed back on her
depths now glowin
the barest hint of c
the same illicit urge

Dear Reader,

I am so excited to share with you my first Harlequin Medical Romance. If recent times have taught us anything, it's how invaluable our medical professionals and health care workers are. I know, from my own past experience as a junior doctor working in various clinical specialties, how patient focused and dedicated hospital staff are as a whole. So, when it came to writing a driven but emotionally withdrawn heroine like Darcy, it was fun to place her in a situation where she could not only discover her worth and shine, but also rattle the hero, sexy surgeon boss Joe, along the way.

Forcing Darcy and Joe to fight hard for their shot at love took them on an emotional journey where they overcome their pasts, finding inner strengths and happiness together.

I hope you enjoy their story.

Love,

JC x

FORBIDDEN FLING WITH DR. RIGHT

JC HARROWAY

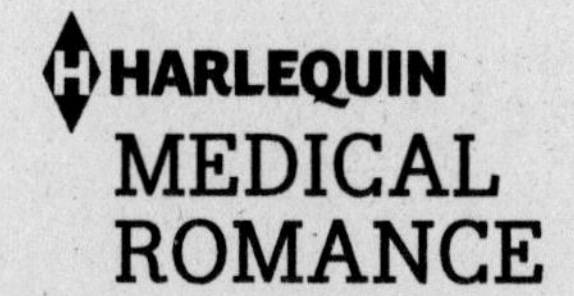

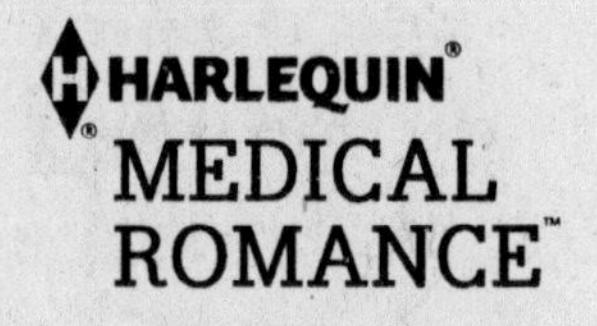

Recycling programs for this product may not exist in your area.

ISBN-13: 978-1-335-40922-5

Forbidden Fling with Dr. Right

This edition published by arrangement with Harlequin Books S.A.

For questions and comments about the quality of this book, please contact us at CustomerService@Harlequin.com.

Harlequin Enterprises ULC
22 Adelaide St. West, 41st Floor
Toronto, Ontario M5H 4E3, Canada
www.Harlequin.com

Printed in U.S.A.

Lifelong romance addict **JC Harroway** took a break from her career as a junior doctor to raise a family and found her calling as a Harlequin author instead. She now lives in New Zealand and finds that writing feeds her very real obsession with happy endings and the endorphin rush they create. You can follow her at jcharroway.com and on Facebook, Twitter and Instagram.

Books by JC Harroway

Forbidden Fling with Dr. Right

is JC Harroway's debut title for Harlequin Medical Romance

Harlequin DARE

Forbidden to Taste
Forbidden to Touch
The Proposition
Bad Business
Bad Reputation
Bad Mistake
Bound to You
Tempting the Enemy

Visit the Author Profile page at Harlequin.com for more titles.

To Dr. H, my own medical hero. Your years of dedication are truly inspirational.

Praise for
JC Harroway

“Temptation at its very best! JC Harroway delights her readers with a forbidden romance and it does not disappoint! I highly recommend this book to anyone who loves a clandestine romance with lots of sparks and so much heart.”

—*Goodreads* on *Bound to You*

CHAPTER ONE

DARCY WRIGHT FIRMLY believed in good impressions, which were never more important than on the first day in a new job. So where the hell was her pen when she needed it? She absently tapped the pocket of her navy-blue surgical scrubs and then scanned the nurses' desk for a stray pen, but no luck. How could she show her new boss what a great surgeon she was when she didn't even have a pen to sign a consent form?

The man would be here any minute and she wanted to wow him, present the sick patient she'd just finished examining, who urgently needed surgery.

Her career, helping people and easing suffering, was the most important thing in her life and her new boss, Joe Austin, was the last thing standing between Darcy and her career pinnacle: being a consultant, important enough to be ultimately responsible for the patients under her care.

'Mr Clarke in room three will be going to Theatre today,' she told Isha, the staff nurse behind the desk. 'If I had something to write with, I'd consent him…' Darcy blew the hair that had escaped her ponytail from her forehead, her flustered search for a pen amplifying her concern for the most seriously unwell of Mr Austin's patients. Of *her* patients.

Isha nodded, took a pen from her uniform pocket and waved it in Darcy's direction.

'Thanks,' Darcy said with a grateful smile.

'Hold on,' said Isha. 'You're adding a patient to Mr Austin's theatre list without asking him first?' Her wide-eyed, slightly impressed smile made Darcy's surgeon senses flicker into high alert.

'Of course… I'm his registrar. That's part of my job.' She added her signature to the operation consent form with a flourish and passed the pen back to Isha.

The other woman's concerned expression fanned Darcy's nerves. Until thirty minutes ago she'd never heard of Joe Austin. She'd expected the kindly older surgeon, Mr Fletcher, who'd interviewed her for this post at London's City Hospital. Instead, she'd discovered that he'd recently retired and she'd been reassigned to Mr Austin's team.

Unease now slithered down Darcy's spine, her good impression under threat. 'Why…what's Mr Austin like?' she asked the wary nurse, her defensive hackles rising. Surely her diligence in arriving early and identifying a patient with an acute abdomen from those admitted overnight would only earn his praise. Or would this boss replacement want to vet every decision she made, as if she were incompetent?

Darcy dismissed the suggestion with a shake of her head. She worked hard for her patients, worked hard to prove she was good at her job. Proving herself was something of a habit, a hang-over from parts of her childhood…

Surely her boss would see her dedication the minute they met.

'Hmm… All the patients love him,' Isha said. 'Even the married ones, if you know what I mean.' She grinned and winked and then typed a flurry of words on the keyboard. 'Haven't you heard of him?'

Isha's eyes sparkled with worrying mischief that tightened Darcy's now frankly anxious stomach.

Heard of him…? How formidable could he be? Did he tear the arms off his registrars for fun?

'No-o-o…' She stretched out the word as her mind raced. 'Until I arrived this morning, I assumed I'd be working for Mr Fletcher… Why would I have heard of him?'

'Oh, my…' said Isha with cryptic glee. 'Are *you* in for a treat. He's no Mr Fletcher looks-wise, that's for sure. Plus, he's an awesome surgeon and kind of famous.'

While Darcy stared with growing dread, Isha's eyes darted sideways to the ward's entrance. 'And here he comes,' she added under her breath.

Darcy's body entered panic mode. She kept her eyes in front, battled the temptation to turn around and gawp at this fearsome creature who, it seemed, might be easy on the eye but might not find her enthusiasm all that impressive given her current state: floundering—no pen, no inkling as to the credentials of her *famous* boss and no time to probe Isha for more than the vague clues the nurse had already offered.

But surely all that mattered was the wellbeing of their patients, first and foremost Mr Clarke.

'Don't tell him that I've never heard of him,' she hissed at Isha in a frantic whisper. Her first impression was not the time to make a professional faux pas. Isha winked and tapped the side of her nose reassuringly, as if to say she'd conceal Darcy's ignorance.

She'd known the nurse for thirty minutes, long enough to discern a dry sense of humour she couldn't help but warm to. Could she be winding Darcy up? Please let this be a joke. The last thing Darcy needed was for her new boss to be some sort of bad-tempered ogre who'd make her job, the one thing she took pride in, miserable.

Darcy's fingers twitched to straighten her wayward ponytail, but she didn't want to be seen to preen. Instead, she snatched the precious seconds to prepare, brace herself mentally for this unexpected man she'd be working closely alongside for the next three months.

Then every tiny hair on her body prickled to attention as she caught a hint of delicious aftershave and sensed an impressively tall and compelling presence at her side.

'Morning, Mr Austin,' said Isha, smiling in welcome at the man in Darcy's peripheral vision.

'Good morning, Isha.' His deep voice resonated with authority despite his personal question. 'Is your daughter over her cold?'

As she could no longer avoid it, Darcy looked up at the formidable new arrival, his handsome profile doing little to settle her frayed nerves. Not an ogre after all. Smartly dressed in a navy three-piece suit, a dove-grey shirt and a burgundy tie, Joe Austin seemed reassuringly confident, with the sort of commanding air that made people hang on his every word. Tall, dark and chiselled, he could be a hotshot financial trader or a male model instead of a gastrointestinal surgeon. Perhaps that was why he was famous—he moonlighted for the top fashion houses…

A flicker of relief shot through Darcy. Despite Isha's scaremongering, Darcy imagined they'd soon come to respect each other, develop a mutually appreciative working relationship.

As if finally noticing her, his gaze swooped over Darcy.

Caught off-guard, Darcy smiled—a twitching grimace generated by his impressive presence. Under his observation, Darcy revised her opinion.

Not handsome—*hot*.

She needn't have bothered with the smile. Before she could open her mouth to introduce herself, he dismissed Darcy without acknowledgement and returned his attention to Isha.

Not a good sign.

All of Darcy's hidden insecurities, honed during a lifetime of feeling not quite good enough, writhed in the pit of her stomach like a bad case of gastric flu while nurse and surgeon conversed for a few moments as if she didn't exist. Darcy pulled herself upright; she was a thirty-one-year-old woman, for goodness' sake. She'd give Joe Austin the benefit of the doubt this once. After all, as Isha had hinted, he was jaw-droppingly attractive.

Waiting for her chance to interrupt, she used the time to observe the man the way a dieter examined chocolate cake.

He was nothing like the genial, rugged-faced Mr Fletcher, who was the far side of sixty and more of a granddad type, that was for sure. Joe's dark untamed hair sported just enough grey at the temples to promise future membership of the 'silver fox' club, and his decadent, almost sensual mouth looked as if the pinched scowl it wore when he'd glanced Darcy's way was borrowed for the occasion.

A groan filled Darcy's head. She had more pressing matters than finding the boss so good-looking that her ovaries bounced with unrestrained glee. She had an urgent case to present: Mr Clarke and his ruptured appendix. Seizing her moment during the briefest lull in his conversation with Isha, Darcy stuck out her hand in his direction.

'Mr Austin…' She was done being ignored.

Her boss turned his head and this time their eyes locked. His were conker-brown, sharp and intense.

Unease and fascination fought for control of Darcy's racing pulse. Seriously… No wonder every female staff member and patient within head-swivelling distance had a smile on their face.

'This is your new registrar,' Isha said, because Darcy seemed to have forgotten that she was a qualified surgeon, not a starry-eyed medical student on her first day on the wards, drooling at the *real* doctor.

Darcy's face ached with the effort of holding an expectant smile in place, the first impression stakes even higher now she knew that she'd be working for someone so renowned.

'Ahh…' he said, clearly unimpressed by what he saw, perhaps her wonky ponytail or her lack of a pen.

What…? She wasn't expecting a fanfare of welcome or fireworks, but he could at least be civil. If it weren't for her tendency to become overly defensive when uncomfortable or judged, she'd let him have a piece of her mind, famous brilliant surgeon or not.

He finally took her proffered hand. 'Good to meet you.' He made it sound anything but *good.*

Darcy's smile offered a final uncertain wobble before dying altogether. How could she have possibly upset him this early into their working relationship? Unless he'd noticed the way she'd checked him out…

Years ago, Darcy had developed a firm and decisive handshake in order to encourage people to take her seriously. She employed it now; she'd never needed it more. 'Darcy Wright. So pleased to meet you, too.'

She dragged in a preparatory breath, ready to bring him up to speed on Mr Clarke, to dazzle him with her diagnostic skills.

'Welcome to my team.' He returned the gesture

with an equally firm touch, his conker-brown eyes both holding her captive and appraising as if she were a virus under a microscope. She pretended to ignore the fact that his words said *Welcome* but his tone asked, *Which rock have you crawled from under?* But she stiffened all the same, the delicious heat of his palm against hers no compensation for what felt like an unfair and hasty evaluation.

Perhaps she'd only imagined the way his eyes seemed to swoop from her head to her toes, forcing her feet to shuffle and her body to shudder as if she'd never been this close to a man before? She dragged her stare from his lush lips, which ridiculously brought to mind desperate kisses. She wasn't here to swoon. So he was hot. Big deal. It was just that it had been a long time, over a year, since she'd found a member of the opposite sex attractive…

Since splitting from her ex, Dean, she'd spent a year in a self-imposed dating hiatus in order to focus on the career she loved. The harder she worked to make a difference to her patients, the greater the personal reward.

She'd always needed to be good at something. She'd embraced her belief that she was the odd one out in her family and learned to stand out. The karate she'd only endured at twelve because her sisters had started ballet class. Or riding her first boyfriend's motorbike during a very brief rebellious teenager phase when even her teachers had written her off. They couldn't see past the make-up and the bad boy boyfriend to bright studious Darcy beneath, who was hurting from the latest slap of rejection from her biological father.

But that had changed as soon as she'd started pushing her pain away and pushing herself instead. Luckily for Joe Austin and Mr Clarke, her drive had brought her here.

Now she had his attention it was time to focus on the patient. 'Can I present Mr Clarke, whom I've added to your urgent theatre list for today?'

Joe raised a sceptical eyebrow, waiting in a loaded silence. His dark stare lacked warmth, or even respect, but its penetrating quality, the length of his sooty lashes and the pounding adrenaline it evoked in Darcy made her so aware of her breathing and the whoosh of her heated blood around her body that she almost lost hold of her determination.

Typical of Darcy that the object of her lust was completely off-limits for a whole raft of reasons…

Her boss.

Probably married.

Seemed to dislike her on sight.

Inside, her hopes for a favourable first impression were rattled. Clearly Isha was right; she should have asked first. They weren't going to be chums, but he was too hot for sense anyway. She would *not* find him attractive. Working for such a guarded man would throw up many challenges she hadn't anticipated without her body reacting every time he looked her way. She needed to show him just how capable she was, not flush every time he addressed her.

'I've acquainted myself with all of your patients,' she said, pushing on regardless. 'Mr Clarke is a thirty-five-year-old man in room three with a perforated appendix who needs surgery. Today.' She handed him the tablet bearing the patient's file, her desire to schmooze her way into his good books dwindling fast. Now she prayed she'd get through her first day without telling him exactly what she thought of him and his hard to please attitude.

Stony-faced, he scrolled through the information. 'Tell me, where did you work before you arrived at City?' His tone implied that he fully expected her answer to be, *Nowhere, I just hung out at the job centre,* as if she wasn't good enough to be *his* registrar.

She opened her mouth to answer, gaping like a goldfish while her insecurities flared to life from the glowing embers she carried inside. Everyone had vulnerabilities, deep-seated fears. Hers stemmed from the childhood belief that she was somehow defective or fundamentally unlovable after her biological father walked out before her first birthday, only reappearing sporadically throughout her childhood, raising and then dashing her hopes that he'd always be a reliable part of her family, of her life.

Darcy was lucky. She had other, more constant family. She loved her half-sisters—Lily, a solicitor, and Stella, the youngest, a doctor too, with whom Darcy shared a flat. She'd had the benefit of equal adoration from her mother and stepfather, Grant, who was a wonderful man. He'd adopted Darcy and treated her just like his biological daughters.

But at times throughout her young life even that hadn't been enough to negate Darcy's feelings of rejection. She'd assumed it must have been something she'd done that drove her father away. If she was well behaved or worked harder at school then she could win back her father's love. Thus began the competitive drive that still pushed her today.

How did this man seem to detect all those insecurities with a single glance? His apparent and unfounded scorn made her blood simmer.

His dismissal was unfair.

In her haughtiest tone, she reeled off a truncated version of her impressive curriculum vitae, her stomach sinking at the tenacity of his blank expression. What *would* it take to impress this man?

'…and before moving to City I worked the surgical rotation at Hanes Hospital with Mr Clough.' She finished with a defiant tilt of her chin, trying to keep the tumult of emotions from her face.

'I know you've inherited rather than chosen me, but Mr Fletcher was delighted to offer me this post,' she said, trying to claw back some outward semblance of the mutually respectful professional relationship she craved, but instead subtly suggesting that the fault lay solely with him and his misplaced prejudices.

'Hmm…' Joe Austin muttered noncommittally as he read Mr Clarke's notes in painstaking detail, as if checking for the mistake that would prove she wasn't a real doctor after all.

The last thing Darcy needed this close to her career's finish line was an arrogant, demanding and ruthless tyrant bossing her around when she'd developed her own way of doing things. Her self-beliefs were constructed on shaky ground as it was without him questioning her professional autonomy. Her career, helping people, fulfilled her and gave her pride.

Clearing her throat, she pushed her agenda, the only real thing that mattered: her patient. 'Mr Austin, I believe Mr Clarke needs an emergency laparotomy.' She kept her tone calm but assertive, her desire to make a good impression buffeted by mounting waves of irritation caused by his impenetrable expression. 'As you can see from his notes, he has obvious signs of an acute abdomen—'

'Have you excluded non-surgical causes for his symptoms?' he interrupted, his gaze still on the screen.

'Of course.' Darcy all but spluttered at his insinuation. Did he think her totally incompetent? It was becoming increasingly difficult to extend him the benefit of the doubt and believe his unwarranted scepticism wasn't personal. She assumed that he must have had lazy trainees in the past. Or perhaps he'd lost a patient recently and had reacted with overbearing distrust. Clearly Joe Austin was unlike any other consultant she'd experienced.

No, he was hotter, but also rude and infuriating.

Darcy dug deep into her reserves of patience. All consultants had their own rules and routines. She'd never before taken it personally. So why now?

Because his attitude made her feel small, inconsequential, an afterthought, the sting too reminiscent of what she'd experienced with her father and, more recently, her ex.

Belatedly, she shot a glance at his left hand,

wondering how his wife put up with him, and found his ring finger to be bare. Damn…that didn't help with the demarcation she was desperately trying to establish between his physical effect on her sad and lonely libido and the way he emotionally seemed to both press all of her soft spots and rile her up until she acted like someone she barely recognised.

She hardened her voice to the authoritative tone she reserved for inebriated relatives in Accident and Emergency on a Saturday night. 'When you examine Mr Clarke, you will see that he has guarding and rebound tenderness in the right iliac fossa.' She reeled off a list of typical signs and symptoms, her defences so high she'd forgotten that she'd set out to impress her superior. She wasn't used to explaining herself this much, not since she was a junior doctor.

Trust her to land the difficult boss. Was it too much to ask, knowing how hard the journey from naïve medical student to veteran consultant was, that he'd show her a modicum of respect and acceptance?

She shoved her hands into the pockets of her white coat with finality in answer to the blank assessing expression he wore as well as his suit. This was about what was best for the patient.

'He has textbook peritonitis,' she continued, her tone now as frosty as his, all expectations abandoned. 'My diagnosis is a ruptured appendix, so I've commenced intravenous antibiotics and consented him for Theatre.' She imagined the satisfying image of Joe Austin's grovelling expression when she proved that her diagnosis was correct in the operating theatre. 'I'm happy to operate if you have a full list.'

Something like momentary respect flashed in Joe's dark eyes, gone as soon as it appeared. Darcy winced at the way that second of recognition lit up her nervous system like a zap of forty thousand volts of electricity.

His lips tightened. 'Ms Wright…' He said her name with that bite of command, only instead of riling her up it made her breath catch and her heart race with the same excitement and anticipation she experienced with a scalpel in her hand.

'If and when,' he added pointedly, 'I'm happy for you to operate on my patients, I'll let you know.'

Darcy spluttered, dumbfounded. 'But I've done this procedure many times in the past.' The brush-off stung, even as she respected his dedication to ensure the care of his patients. Yes, she was new and yet to demonstrate her talents, but she hadn't printed a fake medical diploma from the internet and walked in off the street. She'd trained hard for the past ten years. Made personal sacrifices in order to achieve her goals. While most of her school friends were married, some of them with children, some of them bosses or running their own companies, she still had her training wheels on, both professionally and definitely in her drab private life.

'Let's start the ward round with Mr Clarke, shall we,' Joe said briskly to Isha without acknowledging Darcy's comments and set off down the ward.

Isha, who looked as if she'd won the hospital gossip lottery, shot Darcy a sympathetic but encouraging smile and hurried after the great man.

Insufferable man, more like.

What the hell just happened? Would she have to prove herself worthy over and over again?

Darcy scurried to catch up, feeling like an imposter. Excluded. Maligned. It had been a while since she'd allowed anyone to make her feel that way.

Only the memory of Mr Clarke's pain-induced pallor and clinical signs of peritonitis stiffened Darcy's resolve. Her diagnosis was correct. Joe Austin would soon discover that for himself when he examined the patient. Then he'd have to apologise—publicly, profusely and preferably on his knees.

CHAPTER TWO

JOE AUSTIN DREADED the first day with a new team of trainees. They came with bad or lazy habits they'd acquired working for less demanding bosses than him, habits he'd need to quickly and thoroughly quash. Not that he'd ever met a trainee as downright pushy and defensive as Darcy Wright.

'I'm not sure how they did things at St Mary's, Ms Wright,' Joe said as his long stride made short work of the ward corridor, 'but here at City my patients are *my* responsibility.'

He glanced sideways in time to catch the faint rush of colour to her cheeks. Damn, he'd need to check his delivery, ease her in gently to the fact that instead of working for the genial and relaxed Rod Fletcher, she now had a boss with high expectations that he had no intention of slackening.

Joe ran a tight ship out of necessity, predominantly for his emotional sanity. He knew from devastating experience the consequences of inattention. But perhaps he could make some conciliatory remarks so his new registrar realised his inflexible attitude wasn't personal. At least not personal to Darcy.

'Of course,' she said, her determination obvious in the way she hurried to keep up. 'But it's my job to evaluate your patients.' She wasn't going to accept his explanation at face value, and he couldn't help but respect her for the qualities that made her question.

'Little did I know,' she continued, 'that trying to do my job would earn me a humiliating and very public reprimand.' She ended with a defiant tilt of her chin.

His eyes met hers, an uncomfortable collision on multiple scores. She was inconveniently beautiful and, from his first impressions, sharply intelligent and highly driven. From the first moment he'd looked at her she also roused something in him he hadn't felt in a long time. Enthusiasm, interest, a gravitational pull.

His head still reeled from its effects. He'd spent so long living in a thick, dense fog of grief that any positive feeling was notably astounding.

How had she done that so effortlessly?

'My apologies if I made you feel chastised,' he said, marvelling at the way challenge lit silvery sparks in her brilliant blue irises. 'I'm afraid that, as my registrar, you'll have to grow used to my peculiar little ways.' Even to his own ears he sounded far from apologetic.

But he'd already deduced that this particular registrar would present many tests, not least of all the way she'd rapidly slid under his skin.

She pressed her lush lips together as if she had no intention of granting forgiveness.

'I don't mean to be gruff,' he continued, outlining his expectations for their working relationship, 'but I do demand the highest standards.'

And, like most perfectionists, Joe required the most of himself.

'That's great.' Her smile glittered with resolve. 'Because I'm passionate about my work. I take caring for others very seriously, I put in the hours and, in this case, I know my diagnosis is correct.'

He stopped outside room three and tugged a pair of latex gloves from the box attached to the wall. An admiring smile pulled at his mouth. 'I'm glad to hear that—there are no slackers on my team.'

True to form, she practically spluttered at his insinuation.

'Mr Austin—' she spoke through a clenched jaw '—I, of course, respect your authority, and I'm here to learn from you, but in my previous positions I've worked with a great degree of autonomy. My former consultants were only too happy to leave the routine ward work and patient pre-op prep to me so they could focus on their theatre lists and clinics.'

At least she'd cut the combative tone from her voice somewhat.

Joe nodded. She'd made a perfectly reasonable observation. That was how he too had once worked. Before his personal life fell apart and his job became his only solace. Back then he'd been self-absorbed, too focused on his work to see what was happening at home, with his family.

And he'd paid the ultimate price.

'You have the benefit of an experienced registrar before you.' Darcy ploughed on. 'There's no point keeping a dog and barking yourself, as it were...' she finished with a smile that hinted at her playful sense of humour.

It transformed her face so that Joe took a second look. She wasn't merely beautiful, she was stunning. What would she look like in her own clothes and with her hair down? She certainly rocked a pair of shapeless surgical scrubs, alluring curves in all the right places.

'I agree to a point, Ms Wright,' he said with the calm but inflexible authority he didn't usually need to work at, but with this woman he'd have to stay on his toes. 'But when it's my scalpel, my name next to the patient, *I* need to decide who goes onto my operating list.'

He sighed internally, realising belatedly that

he should ask her to call him Joe. But the thought made his skin prickle with heat, as if the formality of 'Mr Austin' somehow kept her abundant feminine appeal at bay, kept him distant.

No matter he was her senior. Responsible only for her training and education. He couldn't think of her any other way. He definitely shouldn't think about the brilliance of that warm, open, briefly glimpsed smile when she'd greeted him earlier and the way the minute he'd driven it away with his grief-induced foul mood he'd craved a second look.

'Are Mr Clarke's observations stable?' He directed his question to Isha, who'd watched this unusual battle of wills with amused delight.

'He's tachycardic and pyrexial, but his blood pressure is stable.'

'But I've seen patients like him deteriorate rapidly before,' said Darcy, fighting not to be excluded from the conversation. 'I think that once you've examined Mr Clarke you'll agree with my evaluation.'

Why did she need to be right? Why did he care so much about her ego?

'Perhaps I will,' he said, shoving her attractiveness aside as irrelevant, 'but I'm an uncompromising boss. I like things done *my* way. I'll likely double-check everything, so you'd best get used to it.'

Darcy eagerly stepped closer and reached for her own pair of gloves. 'I'm a fast learner, as you'll see when you allow me to operate on Mr Clarke.'

She just didn't give up.

'My CV outlines my extensive surgical log,' she continued, 'and if you don't feel comfortable taking my word for it, you're welcome to supervise the operation.'

'We'll see,' he said, her determination earning his grudging respect. Would they butt horns professionally the entire time? Without stopping to question why a part of him relished the possibility, he focused on the bigger part that needed the order and precision of his work to compensate for the mess he'd made of what had once been an idyllic life as he pushed open the door and strode confidently into the room to greet Mr Clarke.

Her diagnostic skills had proved highly attuned.

Joe blinked in the harsh operating theatre lights and swallowed a wave of guilt at the way he'd reacted negatively to his new registrar. He watched her prepare the surgical field, her long, glossy blonde hair concealed under the blue head covering, with the exception of a few tantalising wisps.

'Ready?' He looked up, bombarded anew by the flash of distrust in Darcy's bright blue eyes.

Fringed with impossibly long eyelashes, her resolute stare was the only part of her face visible above the surgical mask. He should have gone a little easier on her. Theirs was not a career that tolerated hesitancy or insecurity. Had Darcy failed to diagnose the severity of this patient's condition, he might be sitting on the ward right now with life-threatening septicaemia.

She'd done well, and it wasn't her fault that this was a particularly difficult week for him personally.

The impending leukaemia fundraiser he and his ex-wife held twice a year in memory of their daughter Rosie sliced open his poorly healed wound the way he slashed through sutures. It meant well-intentioned friends asking how he was, as if the devastating emotions of losing your only child and then watching helplessly while your marriage imploded could be encompassed by a single socially acceptable word: *fine*.

If he smiled at acquaintances the guilt sliced him in two. If he showed any kind of emotion in front of Laura, his ex-wife, she'd get that glassy look to her eyes and then she'd sniff and fight tears. Then the grief, for which there was no shelf life or miraculous cure, would crush him from the inside until all he could do was wait for their guests to leave and pound the punch bag hanging in his garage until his knuckles bled and exhaustion took him to unconsciousness.

He'd spent many a night asleep on the concrete floor over the years, waking with swollen hands—the irreplaceable tools he needed to work—and swollen eyes.

No wonder meeting his unexpectedly beautiful and assertive registrar had thrown him off course. If only the balm of her attractiveness, both physical and intellectual—a likely consequence of his non-existent dating life since his divorce—wasn't completely irrelevant.

She nodded. 'Are you happy for me to proceed, Mr Austin?'

'Please continue, Ms Wright.' He stifled a sigh, dark thoughts of his past failures abolishing the foolish flickers of desire.

'You're sighing.' Darcy paused from preparing the patient's abdomen, frustration evident in the tone of her voice. 'Have I done something wrong? Is there another way, i.e. your way, that you'd like me to prepare the field?'

She'd swabbed the skin with iodine and demarcated the area with sterilised surgical drapes in a perfectly standard manner. And with swift precision that told him she had no intention of altering her technique to mollify his peculiar whim.

He cleared his throat. 'No. I was distracted by a…personal matter. Carry on.'

Darcy gave a momentary pause where she observed him intently. Then she continued.

Joe breathed again. He needed to get himself together. At this rate she'd think he was unhinged or easily preoccupied.

'While we're on the subject of doing things my way,' he said from behind his own surgical mask, 'I want you to ensure that the new foundation doctors run a blood test for pancreatitis on all of my patients admitted with abdominal pain. I have a standing rule.'

Thorough routines—another technique he used to restore some sense of order and control to his shattered existence. Ticking every box, giving his job his whole, somehow absolved a minuscule fraction of his guilt for the way he'd lost what mattered the most: his family. First his daughter and then his marriage. Because without his work who was he?

Not a husband and no longer a father.

'Of course.' Darcy nodded, her keen stare wary and suspicious. 'I, too, never pick up a scalpel until I've seen the pancreatic enzyme levels and excluded all non-surgical causes of abdominal pain,' she stated calmly, her tone full of reproof. 'The first consultant I ever worked for taught me *that*.'

Joe winced behind his mask. Perhaps he did sound a little patronising to someone of her experience. Although her implication reminded him he likely had little to teach her beyond how to become a paranoid workaholic, he couldn't help but applaud her calm persistence. She was at least ten years younger than his forty-three, and people rarely challenged his authority in the workplace.

To the casual outsider, he was the mighty Joe Austin after all, the once golden boy of gastro-intestinal surgery, now a jaded and bereft shell of his former self.

He cleared his throat. 'I've seen acute pancreatitis missed before, confused for a surgical emergency.' Yes, this was rookie surgeon stuff that she already knew, but his high standards, his reminders and double-checks hurt no one and were, in fact, designed to do the opposite: keep his patients safe and ensure that his daughter's death made some sort of sense, even if only as a distraction technique.

'I won't put any patient of mine through an unnecessary laparotomy,' he said in further explanation, although he couldn't fathom why Darcy's opinion of him mattered in the slightest. Let her think him bad-tempered and demanding.

Except…

Her observant stare seemed to probe his inner thoughts way too clearly. She'd practically told him how to do his job on the ward earlier. Perhaps he cared what she thought of him because he hoped to conceal how much he needed his work—how it gave him purpose and allowed him to focus on others' lives rather than the train wreck of his own.

'On that we agree,' she said, her tone clipped as she adjusted the overhead lights to aid her clear view.

Joe watched her with renewed fascination. Was it just his gruffness that made her defensive, or had she arrived this morning already gunning to push her agenda? He knew all too well the demands of life as a consultant surgeon, and she already had many of the qualities required. Confidence, assertiveness and persistence. The attributes were practically a requirement of a surgeon who made life and death decisions on a daily basis.

But what was her personal story behind the mask? Did she have a husband or boyfriend or children that she hardly saw, the way he'd neglected what mattered most: spending time with his loved ones?

When she caught him staring her eyes hardened, as if she fully expected his interference or criticism.

'What?' she asked, pausing with her hand outstretched for a scalpel. 'Why are you looking at me like that?'

Joe battled the urge to smile. She was so… feisty. Refreshing. Rousing. Her apparent lack of respect for his authority should rankle. Instead, she made him feel…lighter, as if at any moment he might burst into laughter at his own absurdities. When was the last time he'd been gripped by such a spontaneous positive emotion? And what was it about this woman that awoke him to amusement, among other emotions?

He blinked and tried to clear the insanity in his head. He could *not* find his junior colleague attractive, desirable or fascinating. Aside from the ethical barriers, the fact he was her boss and therefore held the balance of power in their professional dynamic, he'd hadn't had a single date since he and Laura split three years ago.

Rusty would be an understatement.

Whenever he'd thought about dating in the past, he couldn't move past how undeserving he was of a second chance after his family's tragedy. He'd had his shot at happily ever after and he'd messed up.

Now, there was only work and keeping fit, both physically and mentally so he could work some more, the cycle rewarding and absorbing but also addictively numbing.

He'd all but given up on those vital parts of his masculinity still functioning but Darcy Wright, with her bright eyes and her dazzling smile, could restore the sex drive of a monk.

'How am I looking at you?' he said, the foreign heat of intrigue shifting through his veins, where normally work was a place to keep busy, to lock down any thought beyond patient care and avoid feeling anything at all.

Darcy huffed. 'As if you're waiting for me to make a mistake.' The briefest flash of vulnerability lit her eyes before she looked down again, focused on their patient.

His gut tightened with renewed regret and something more. Shame. He didn't usually care what anyone thought of his high expectations. Most staff had been around long enough to know the old Joe Austin, the surgeon he'd been before his life fell apart, and cut him the according slack. But unless she'd already had time to catch up on hospital gossip, Darcy didn't know that there'd once been a more relaxed and engaging side to him. That he'd enjoyed a joke with his patients, played soft rock ballads in Theatre while he operated and showed the nurses photos of Rosie—proud dad moments, the memory of which now turned his stomach.

Perhaps if he'd been at home more, he might have noticed her rapid deterioration and Rosie would still be alive. The dull ache of self-hatred somewhere under his ribs grumbled awake like an ill-tempered bear disturbed from hibernation.

Of course, none of this was Darcy's fault and he'd need to apologise.

Shoving his feelings of inadequacy back down, he returned to their conversation. 'It's my job to observe your technique, supervise and evaluate you in preparation for your next job as a consultant.' A good reminder to stave off those wayward moments of attraction.

'I know,' she said, sounding completely unconvinced, 'but there's observation and then there's *observation*.' She handed the scalpel to the theatre nurse and asked for a forceps.

His lips twitched once more beneath his mask. 'Am I making you uncomfortable?' Interesting... Had he rattled her as much as she'd unnerved him? Would her time working for him be filled with these...sparks?

'Not in the slightest,' she said, but her evasive stare said otherwise. 'Are we still good?' Darcy asked the anaesthetist, checking that the patient's level of anaesthesia was satisfactory.

Joe deserved the dressing-down he suspected she'd held back after the way he'd grilled her on the ward. Old habits reared their heads, and his gloved hands itched to take over control of the instruments. Her confident incision on Mr Clarke's abdomen was textbook—right over Mc-

Burney's point, the anatomical landmark for the location of the appendix. He agreed with her diagnosis: peritonitis secondary to a likely ruptured appendix. He'd expect a trainee with her experience to easily recognise and treat the surgical emergency.

So why had he been so hard on her?

Because he hadn't expected Darcy herself. Her tenacity, her determination, her spirit had made him take a second look beyond his first impression. And then a third and fourth look. She'd roused him from emotional detachment, made him feel something after years of trying to feel nothing. He hadn't cared about anything beyond his work, his patients, for so long that the emotion—any positive emotion—felt…alien, as if it was her probing him with uncomfortable questions, not the other way around. With his guard erected, he'd gone overboard in questioning her diagnosis.

'You didn't say I told you so,' he said as the collection of pus making the otherwise fit and healthy Mr Clarke sick came into view through the small incision she'd made.

Her eyes clashed with his in surprise, quickly replaced by resignation. 'I want a glowing reference when I leave, not to score petty points.'

Her tone was clipped with concentration, her movements precise and practised in a way that told Joe she possessed that innate instinct which turned a skilled technician into an intuitive surgeon.

'Besides,' she added, 'I'm here to learn from you so that I can be the best surgeon I can be. Maybe even as good as you.'

Joe said nothing. He'd once shared Darcy's ambition, and he still did to a degree, only now his motives were as much about self-preservation as they were about wanting to save the world one sick patient at a time. His perfectionism had become another shield he used to ward off regret.

'I'll teach you everything I can.' Although, he'd learned life's most valuable lesson outside the hospital, the hard way—a lesson he would wish on no one.

'I look forward to it,' she said. 'Although, I didn't realise that I'd be working for someone so notable when I arrived on the ward this morning.'

He winced—he most certainly didn't deserve her awe. She obviously knew of his work in the development of the RA Clip, a now universally used surgical clip that cut the risk of post-operative bleeding in half.

Yes, he was good at one thing: his job. But he'd been a largely absent father and, at the end, an inadequate husband. He'd once had it all. But he'd ruined it all, too. Did Darcy know about Rosie's death, about his failure as a father, the only truly important role he'd ever had?

'I've designed a surgical clip, not cured cancer.' Joe's insides twisted with familiar remorse as surely as if Darcy were probing inside his abdomen, not their patient's. If only he *could* have cured cancer. He might still have his darling little girl…

Nausea swirled in his gut, resurrecting the intrusive thoughts that plagued him day and night. He'd once been so busy treating others at the hospital that he hadn't been home when his daughter's health had rapidly deteriorated four years ago, following a short illness he'd thought was common viral gastroenteritis. By the time his wife and six-year-old daughter had arrived at the hospital Rosie had been unconscious from a brain haemorrhage—a rare complication of her undiagnosed acute leukaemia—and admitted to intensive care. He'd missed his chance to speak with his beloved girl one last time. To remind her that he loved her and always would.

A wave of grief slashed through the sutures barely holding his heart together, the pain snatching his breath away. He should have noticed something was seriously wrong. He was a doctor. Observation, intuition, diligence were vital parts of his role. He'd let Rosie down. There was no going back to save her. God knew he'd prayed hard enough for that impossible second chance—one he didn't deserve.

'Well, as you can see, I'm a perfectly competent surgeon and you're going to have to trust me a tiny bit if you ever plan on sleeping again.' She deftly directed the scrub nurse's suction to where she wanted it. 'We're on call tonight—it's going to be a long shift if you insist on shadowing every move I make, double-checking things a medical student can do unaided.'

She was right. He had plenty to do.

'I'm sure that my little foibles seem…overcautious.' Helping his patients allowed him to focus anywhere other than on his own messed-up head and tattered heart. 'But you do seem to have things under control.'

While he'd been half overseeing, half ruminating on his failures, Darcy had cleared the abscess collected around Mr Clarke's appendix and tied off the artery in preparation for removing the perforated structure.

'Thank you, I think…' Her lips twitched under her mask with what he guessed was a sardonic smile. After years of working with the face coverings he'd become adept at reading people's eyes. She adjusted the retractor to open up the wound. 'Now you can see that I'd never allow professional awe or first day nerves or even self-doubt distract me from a patient's diagnosis or care.'

Her subtext added, *Even when my senior colleague gets in the way.*

Self-doubt? She seemed extremely confident. She'd given him what-for, hadn't she?

The scrub nurse held out a clamp. On instinct, Joe reached for it at the exact same moment as Darcy. Their gloved hands collided, the brush of her fingers against his, followed swiftly by the locking of their stares.

Awareness permeated the sterile atmosphere as they stood face to face, hands frozen, his atop hers, on the handle of the surgical instrument.

It could only have lasted a split second, but it was enough time to flood Joe's body with the same restless heat he'd experienced when she'd first turned to smile at him this morning on the ward.

He'd had to suppress the feeling then, as he must now.

He relinquished the clamp and Darcy recovered first. 'I'm more than happy to finish up with Mr Clarke alone. Unless you have any last advice?' Darcy asked, hinting that it was high time he left her to operate unaided.

The feeling of her fingers under his persisted, forcing him to gather all of his best coping strategies. 'Just a mantra I find useful: mistakes cost lives.'

'They do,' she agreed, her blue eyes softening with the compassion of their profession. 'Although, inevitably, we can't save every patient. That's a reality of the job, isn't it?'

Damn, he didn't need her seeing him so intuitively. He didn't need this…distraction. And yet she brought his emotions, good and bad, to the surface with her smile and her grit and her… dogged persistence.

He offered a single brisk nod that made his neck feel like a brittle log about to crack and splinter. 'I'll leave you to it then…' Like it or not, he couldn't oversee every aspect of patient care himself. There weren't enough hours in the day, and God knew he'd tried to fill every second as an antidote to being alone with himself. With his vicious thoughts and weighty regrets.

For now, he needed Darcy as much as she needed him.

'I'll be next door dictating letters if you want me.' Joe left the theatre, disposing of his gloves, mask and gown, wishing he could dispose of his remorse as easily.

Here in the confines of the hospital where he'd lived out the worst day of his life, he'd found a modicum of not exactly peace but routine in his life, and that was all he deserved.

No, Darcy Wright was a fascination he couldn't indulge. Not now. Not ever.

CHAPTER THREE

DARCY RETURNED HER toothbrush to her bag and splashed her pale face with cold water. She was used to long sleepless nights on call, but she'd never grown accustomed to the icky dry mouth and gritty eyes of sleep deprivation. It was amazing what a three a.m. mouthful of toothpaste and an invigorating face splash could achieve in lieu of an undisturbed eight-hour sleep.

Almost as invigorating as spending the day and most of the night with the most infuriating man she'd ever met: her control freak boss.

If only she didn't respect his surgical skills and bedside manner so much. If only he was gruff with the patients. But he seemed to come alive when he was helping someone, showing tantalising glimpses of the Joe who was caring, kind and dedicated.

She exhaled, drained by the emotional gamut she'd run since she'd first laid eyes on him the day before. Never had she met someone who simultaneously left her both frustrated and in awe. Who, for every spare second of her long first day, occupied her thoughts in good ways—his skill in the operating theatre and the calm reassuring tone he reserved for his patients—and bad. His ability to push her buttons was unsurpassed and, no matter how many times she told herself it was pointless, ridiculous and, above all, forbidden, she couldn't switch off her attraction.

Fortunately, they'd been too busy with admissions and surgeries for her to dwell on Joe's magnetism and her body's persistent weakness.

Darcy brushed her hair and retied her ponytail, her stomach in knots at the thought of spending the next three months working in close proximity to such an absorbing and exasperating mentor. She could keep her head down, avoid him and ignore the fact that he made sexy look…drab. But if he kept up his hovering and taking over, she might snap and do or say something…stupid.

Darcy's cheeks warmed. If her sisters could see driven, career-minded Darcy now, all rattled and riled by a man, they'd die laughing. Then they'd probably remind her that before her ex, before she'd sworn off dating, Joe was exactly the type of man she'd once fantasised she'd end up with.

'I'm going to marry a builder, like Dad,' said Lily, aged eight.

'I'm going to marry a superhero,' said Stella, aged six.

'I'm going to be a doctor and marry a doctor and live in a castle in Scotland,' said Darcy, aged ten.

Even in childish fantasies she'd felt the need to outshine her sisters and distinguish herself somehow, because she'd grown up uncertain of what she'd done to make her father stay away for increasingly long periods. She'd acted out, imagined a 'them and her' distinction between her sisters that only existed in her head. She'd convinced herself that she must be different if she wasn't even good enough for her own father, who would appear for a wonderful but brief flash and then disappear into the endless passage of time. Darcy never knew when he'd show up again or which of his promised visits he'd keep.

Joe's far from welcoming attitude today had once more brought out those deep-rooted fears of being…inconsequential. Trying to impress such a man would only lead to the kind of heartache she'd experienced over and over as a girl, waiting for the phone to ring. Now, all she hoped was that they could work alongside each other in relative harmony.

Somewhat refreshed, Darcy emerged from the bathroom and came to an abrupt halt. Joe was sprawled on one of the comfy chairs in the theatre staffroom, his hair dishevelled from removing his surgical hat and the fatigue of their long day and night finally haunting his intelligent deep brown eyes.

Her pulse flew. 'Um… Hi, Mr Austin. I thought you'd left,' she said, a rush of compassion hijacking her surprise. His tiredness made him seem more human, more approachable, more real. Positive feelings Darcy wanted to reject and instead question why he hadn't gone home or sloped off to sleep in an on-call room like all her previous consultants.

'I think it's time we use first names, don't you, Darcy?' he said, catching her completely off-guard. 'Is it okay for me to call you Darcy?'

The sound of her name on his lips body-slammed her, robbing her of breath and any hope of coherent conversation.

Every time she succeeded in grappling her opinion of him under control, he morphed again, showing another side of himself, clouding her judgement. Because where yesterday those eyes of his carried nothing but suspicion and distrust, now they seemed haunted by a whole raft of more complex emotions, expressive and open. His tall, lean body—so sexy in his scrubs, which revealed a triangle of dark chest hair, and his powerful arms, corded with muscle—was relaxed. Even his hands were elegant and yet capable in a totally arousing way.

Everything inside Darcy clenched in anticipation. Her head contained a riot of confusing feelings—attraction, exasperation, excitement and exhaustion. But, for all his sex appeal, he was still the man who'd doubted and patronised her all day. She could find him attractive and irritating at the same time.

No—she couldn't find him anything! He was her boss.

'Um… Okay… Joe…' she said in response to his request for informality, his first name intimate on her tongue, sending irrelevant flutters through her belly. 'Do you need me?'

A hint of a roguish smile tugged at his mouth and lit his eyes.

She flushed as she realised that her question sounded…suggestive. More alarming, though, was her insane desire for him to reply 'yes' for all the wrong reasons.

To cover her body's inappropriate, sleep-deprived reaction, she pretended to check her phone for a missed call from Accident and Emergency. All doctors were highly attuned to the sound of a pager or the ringing of their phone—but she needed the valuable seconds to regroup her defences and battle that pesky buzz of attraction that showed no signs of abating, no matter how confounding she found her boss.

'No, I don't need you.' His stare lingered on Darcy as if he had something else momentous to say. It propelled Darcy's frantic pulse to a dizzying new high.

Please, no... The first name thing was shock enough.

'Okay...' she croaked, trying to rein in the physical interest she was certain her weary body couldn't have mustered five minutes ago.

They'd just emerged from a six-hour surgery—a multiple abdominal stabbing case of a man in the wrong alleyway at the wrong time, but fortunately on Joe Austin's watch. Darcy found Joe a fascinating surgeon. He worked with the same dogged precision and minute attention to detail he applied to checking up on her. No blood vessel was too fine to escape cauterisation. No corner or crevice of the abdominal cavity was too obscure to warrant checking. And, unlike Darcy, whose feet and back had ached, leading to the odd fidget and position readjustment, Joe's energy levels had seemed as unwaveringly constant as his concentration and focus.

Their chosen career carried its own unique set of challenges. But the hint of vulnerability she'd seen in his stare when he'd said *'Mistakes cost lives'* was like a shot of curiosity to Darcy's bloodstream. What forces had shaped brilliant and dedicated Joe Austin to be so hyper-vigilant to the point of obsessive? A bad experience? The shock of losing a patient?

And why did she find his intelligence and commitment, even his humanity—on first impressions she'd have declared him incapable of the chink in his armour—the regret she'd spied, so bloody seductive? It would be much easier to dislike everything about him, his overbearing attitude *and* his looks.

'Our stabbing victim is stable and on his way to Intensive Care,' he said.

Darcy sighed, all thoughts of gently enquiring why he was so over-the-top-dedicated evaporating. 'Post-op checks are my job. I just wanted to splash my face with water first.'

He shrugged in explanation and tapped the folder on the seat next to him. 'I went back for my notes.'

Why did his diligence seem to bring all her worst traits to the surface, make her feel…small, somehow not good enough? Was it just admiration for someone she now knew was a surgical legend? Or was it that he didn't seem to see or understand the importance of her career to Darcy, how helping people filled a hole in her heart?

The academic success of her teens came with the kind of praise and accolades that told her that, despite her father's waning interest in her as a daughter, she was okay, good at something. She'd become addicted, her competitive nature blossoming as she chased one success after another. Not that she could have anticipated how fulfilling she'd find a career in medicine.

'Why are you so defensive?' he asked, questioning the shell she used to protect herself when he'd spent the day reminding her of those childhood inadequacies by niggling at the career she took pride in. His expression was infuriatingly steady, as if he had no part to play in erecting her barriers. With a chill that poured through her veins, she realised how effortlessly Joe had jarred defences she'd spent her life fortifying.

But his attitude also reminded her of her ex, Dean's fault-finding, which by the end had felt pretty constant.

'You're rarely home.'

'You work too hard.'

'You put us last.'

Dean was a sculptor. He'd never really understood her drive or career choice, as if wanting to become a surgeon was merely playing at make-believe when the only truly noble endeavour was art. Realising they were headed for angst and heartache, she'd broken off her engagement and made her choice: work.

Joe watched her now, his stare tracing her

flushed features as if she had some fascinating and newly discovered disease. Could he read her mind? Could he sense how she'd failed to balance her career and her one serious relationship?

Instead of answering his inflammatory question, she bit out, 'Why are you so intent on doing *my* job before I have a chance to do it first? You said overcautious, but it comes across as…paranoid, as if you trust no one.'

She pressed her lips together tightly. She shouldn't have said that. She shouldn't have argued with him at all. But the same fatigue she'd seen on his face dragged at her, and he'd been a constant burr beneath her skin since he'd walked onto the ward.

'Paranoid…?' he drawled, quietly serious, eyes disturbingly watchful and glittering with provocation. 'Perhaps it's because I hate learning something the hard way.'

Darcy vibrated with remorse. What lesson had he learned that caused such profound over-vigilance?

Joe narrowed his stare in a way that made Darcy think of a powerful predator, lightning fast and ruthless. 'But I asked first.' He raised his eyebrows, waiting.

Darcy sighed; she had some insight into her pushiness. The pain of repeated rejection from her father over the years had made her self-reliant, out to prove herself. It also made her judgement sensitive and conflict avoidant.

Except with this man, with whom clashes came readily.

'I'm a surgeon,' she said. 'It's my job to be assertive and decisive.' She held his watchful stare pointedly. 'Perhaps *I* hate being underestimated.'

It reminded her that, no matter how hard she tried to be a good daughter, nothing she did helped her to hold onto her father.

She cleared her throat. 'Surely you can see why your tendency to question me as if I'm a novice med student might cause me to be a little...prickly.'

'Noted,' he said, dragging in a prolonged breath and whipping the wind from Darcy's sails. 'Sit down, Darcy.' His face wore a conflicted expression, as if he wanted both her company and to be alone.

She, too, could do with a reprieve from his all-consuming masculinity and the way he seemed to bring out the worst in her.

But as he'd already checked on their last patient she couldn't avoid his order/invitation. But where to sit? Too far away might seem rude, but too close and he might feel crowded, not to mention that she'd end up...distracted.

A small sigh escaped her lips. She was a grown woman for goodness' sake. She wanted nothing to do with her ridiculous…crush. Pulling herself together, Darcy took the seat next to Joe.

Big mistake.

Not only was she close enough for her strung-out senses to detect the subtle spicy tones of his aftershave and body heat, his proximity also reminded her how she'd almost burst into flames when she'd accidentally brushed hands with him in the operating theatre. Time had slowed to a standstill at the connection, a frozen split second where their eyes locked as if seeing each other for the first time all over again. His strong, glove-covered fingers had been warm against hers and, as if defibrillated, Darcy's heartbeat skittered faster than when she'd peered inside the incision in Mr Clarke's abdomen and saw that her diagnosis of a ruptured appendix had been correct, the thrill acute and blinding.

'Why don't you try to get some rest?' she said, newly annoyed by her physical reaction to the man.

Joe shook his head. 'I don't sleep well at the best of times, so there's no point even trying here.'

Something dark shifted in his stare, something she'd seen the first time their eyes had met this morning, only she'd been too caught up in impressing him to attribute the look she now identified: tortured.

Joe Austin was tortured.

By the mistake he was so keen to avoid in future, the bitter lesson he'd learned. All doctors feared losing a patient through some sort of human error.

Darcy swallowed the lump in her throat. The ghost of regret in his eyes called to the part of her that wanted to help people. She still remembered the buzz of caring for her sister, Lily, when she'd broken her leg as a child. She'd felt needed. Valued. It was the first time she'd considered the possibility of becoming a doctor.

But she knew very little about Joe, beyond what she'd gleaned on the internet during a lull in their operating list when she'd snatched a quick sandwich from the cafeteria. Not only famous in the surgical world, Joe was also well-known on the UK celebrity scene as the husband of internationally bestselling fiction author Laura Knight.

Operating on Mr Clarke had cut her fact-finding mission short at that point, his ruptured appendix taking priority over her rampant curiosity and strange and inappropriate dejection.

She forced herself to raise his marital status now. Hopefully it would act as the final nail in the coffin of her preoccupation with him. 'Won't your wife be expecting you at home?'

The same sinking feeling she'd experienced on seeing a photo of the glamorous, beaming Mr and Mrs Joe Austin earlier today swooped in her stomach. Stupid because of course someone like him—handsome, successful, intelligent—would have a beautiful, talented wife.

'I usually spend my on-call nights here, catching up on work.' Joe's stare took on that intensity he wore when he wielded a scalpel. Directed her way, it made Darcy's breathing shallow.

'And I've been divorced for three years.' A hint of amusement tugged at his mouth as he dropped that bombshell as if he'd seen through her lame fishing attempt.

Divorced...

A worrying wave of relief washed through Darcy's veins. He no longer had a beautiful, talented wife.

Poor Joe...

This was bad news for her, too. Off-limits due to his marital status threw up an instant brick wall. But simply off-limits because he was her boss became a much flimsier barrier.

Darcy looked away—there was no way he could ever know about her secret lusting. Professional judgement she could handle, but another personal disaster at this stage in her career...?

No way.

CHAPTER FOUR

'SO WHY DID you choose medicine as a career?' Joe asked, placing an empty coffee mug on the table in front of them.

Darcy's body overheated at the pressure of making conversation with a man who didn't seem to like her in the slightest, perhaps even suspected her inappropriate crush and made her feel like both a siren and a simpleton whose professional input—the one thing in her life she took pride in—was superfluous.

She would have preferred to talk shop, ask him why he'd favoured nylon over silk sutures in the stabbing case, to distract her wayward hormones, which were determined to see him as some sort of sexy doctor pin-up from one of those medical soaps.

'My younger sister broke her leg falling from a trampoline,' she said. 'She was six and I was eight. It was summer, so I spent the school holidays entertaining Lily—fetching her glasses of lemonade, reading to her, scratching her toes and drawing cartoon cats on her plaster cast.' Darcy chuckled at the happy memories, shoving away the recollection of other feelings from that summer. She was supposed to have gone on holiday to France with her father, their first holiday together. She'd been looking forward to it with giddy glee, dancing around the house with excitement and probably annoying her parents with a constant barrage of questions. Then he'd cancelled out of the blue, two days before he was due to collect Darcy.

She could still hear her mother's end of the ensuing tense telephone conversation and how her mother's obvious annoyance with the man who'd flitted in and out of Darcy's life had somehow increased Darcy's disappointment. It had been the first time her blind adoration for her larger-than-life father wavered, her heart breaking, confused over what she'd done wrong. It had also set in motion years of Darcy trying and failing to regain the closeness she'd felt for her father as a young girl, years of seeking his attention, battling the guilt she felt for loving Grant, as if she was somehow betraying her *real* father.

'I liked nursing Lily so much, I knew I wanted to help people,' she said, aware of Joe's continued observation while her insides were so raw.

'What about you?' She tried to brush off the

claws of those childhood demons. 'Did you always imagine you'd be a surgeon?'

'My mother was a nurse.' He shrugged as if that explained everything.

Darcy wanted more. Her brain bombarded her with questions to which she wanted answers: *What happened to cause your divorce? Have you moved on? Do you have any children?*

Then he changed tack. 'I took your advice and reread your CV earlier.'

'Oh…?' Darcy smiled. So he knew her academic accomplishments and her employment pedigree. Perhaps he'd respect her professionally after all. Perhaps their disastrous first day was a blip. Hopefully, without the emotional ups and downs—nerves, the pressure to impress and him chipping away at her confidence—her silly infatuation would evaporate. Before she knew it, she'd be applying for a consultant post with Joe's glowing endorsement.

'I was particularly interested to see you were featured in that TV show—the one that followed a cohort of medical students through university and into their first job. I watched a clip after our ward round this morning.'

Chills doused Darcy, as if she'd dived into the Arctic Ocean. 'Did you?' She clenched her jaw and looked away.

Just when she thought she'd earned a few

crumbs of his respect, he seemed to be taking a subtle dig at one of her bad choices. She only kept that show on her CV because the series had gone on to win several TV awards in the reality category, but she'd grown to regret her participation. In her first year at medical school she'd naively signed up, thinking it would help her to stand out from the crowd and a fun way to document the start of her career. Except some of the early episodes showed her and her fellow students letting their hair down. Darcy hadn't taken herself as seriously back then as she did now. She'd been young, uncertain of who she was because she'd recently reached out to her father again, in the hope of forging an adult relationship now that she was a daughter he could surely be proud of.

She'd called him out of the blue, taken the train to Edinburgh, where he'd settled, her heart so full of hope that he'd want to have an adult relationship with his daughter that she could barely breathe. What she'd discovered had torn that foolish heart in two. He had two more daughters. It wasn't that he hadn't wanted a child; he just hadn't wanted Darcy enough to stay in her life.

Young, newly away from the security of home and heartbroken by her father's ultimate act of betrayal, she'd acted out, developed a bit of a reputation as the party girl of the show. The director had delighted in portraying her as the flaky one, not really there to become a doctor. But she'd quickly learned that wasn't who she was. That her father wasn't who she'd hoped he'd be. That she could neither impress him nor make him love her.

Some blinkers could never be replaced once they were removed, and she'd stopped reaching out to him.

Since then, she'd worked hard and made it through med school and earned her job as registrar to the mighty and famous Joe Austin…

Who, of course, would put her in her place, focus on a time from her past that made her seem…frivolous and attention-seeking, when in reality she'd been desperate to prove she deserved to be at medical school, that she'd work harder and longer than the next student to show her father that she could do anything, be anything, even without him.

Darcy's hackles rose to new heights. Of course, Joe wouldn't compliment her research on cirrhosis patients or the fact that she'd presented her scientific paper at the Surgical Advances and Innovations Forum to a delegation of eight hundred in the field last year. He'd formed opinions about her even before they'd met, perhaps because he hadn't chosen her himself. He'd made it clear that he didn't think she was good enough, didn't want her. Why else would he give her such an undeserved hard time? He'd insinuated she was slack about her work, someone he needed to watch closely for mistakes and check up on.

If she hadn't been awake for more than seventeen hours she might have slept on her conclusions, modified her tone, even bitten her tongue.

'If you've read my CV then you know that I take my work seriously. As seriously as you do, in fact,' she said, levelling him with an unflinching stare. She must have sounded highly strung, but Joe's condescending reminder of something she wasn't totally proud of brought her repressed frustrations and the fear of not being good enough to the surface.

'I didn't know it was a touchy subject.' Joe winced, looking immediately contrite.

But it was too late for Darcy, who'd tolerated him hovering and questioning the most basic of her decisions. She wouldn't accept him putting her down after the years of hard work and the sacrifices she'd made for her chosen career.

'You know, I've tried my best to impress you and show you that I'm responsible and diligent and competent in caring for your patients.' With her reserves of resilience against his criticisms drained, Darcy muttered, 'Now I understand the divorce…'

Heat raced up her neck and flooded her face. She'd never before spoken to a senior colleague, or any colleague, like that. What was she doing? She'd sabotage this position and any reference he might give her in the future. She'd blown it within her first twenty-four hours on the job.

She clamped her hand over her mouth, ashamed of her rudeness. She blamed fatigue and stress or her tendency to be prepared for an attack. She'd had a long, emotionally fraught day. Clearly, she wasn't thinking or acting straight.

'Now who's making assumptions?' he replied before she could apologise. 'My marital failure is none of your business.' He leaned forward in his seat so his stare sparked with hers. 'Are *you* in a relationship?' His gaze fell to her left hand, where she'd once worn Dean's engagement ring.

Clearly, she'd touched a nerve, too.

She opened her mouth to tell him, to explain herself, but he ploughed on.

'Have you successfully managed to combine an intense and demanding career with a blissful personal life?' His mouth flattened into a terse line.

For one euphoric second his probing personal question, his interest in her marital status, made her wonder if he was as fascinated by her as she was by him, until she recalled her humiliation and sense of failure when she'd realised that she hadn't been able to make her personal life a success, that she and Dean were incompatible. She'd once thought she'd had it all. The career she'd always wanted. An understanding fiancé. But it hadn't lasted. Dean's support had dwindled as Darcy's hours grew longer, the exams harder, the stresses more absorbing. She'd had nothing in common with his friends and their differences had seemed to amplify in importance as time went by until she'd felt like the outsider the young Darcy had feared she was.

'No, you're right. I've been single for a year.' Darcy braced her hands on the arms of the chair and swivelled her body to face him. 'I put my career first before my fiancé and I called it off. That same career you seem to be implying that I neither deserve nor value. But, as I see it, we have at least one thing in common—we're both married to our work.'

A glimmer of respect hovered in Joe's steely stare. 'I never said you didn't deserve your career. Of course—'

'You've doubted me at every turn,' she interrupted, her pulse flying as they faced off. 'You know, I never expected us to become friends, but I at least hoped you'd respect my work ethic and the long hard years of dedication and sacrifice I've invested to reach this stage in my career. You know what I've done to get here, because you've done it, too.'

She ignored his deep frown. Ignored the warning bells that she'd made her point and said enough.

'You may not like me, Mr Austin,' she said, returning to their earlier formality, 'but we're very similar, you and I. We put our patients first. We put in the hours. Perhaps because neither of us has anything else in our life…'

Her harsh words hung in the stiff silence. The tense seconds in the wake of her outrageously rude accusations made Darcy's breath come in incensed pants. He too was breathing hard, his dark eyes locked with her blue ones.

Had she flushed her career down the drain? She'd likely lose her job.

And yet a current of suspense hung in the air, tendrils of energy snaking between them, sparks of heat and fire.

Darcy's indignation became swamped by the absurd urge to kiss Joe's arrogant sculpted mouth. It made no sense, apart from the fatigue surely clouding her judgement, the unfairness of her current situation and a sick sense of self-sabotage.

If she was going to be sacked, she might as well go out with a bang, end her terrible first day, perhaps even her long-coveted career, on *her* terms, not his. Payback for him making her doubt herself all over again when she was within spitting distance of her consultant job and the security of her own achievements.

She could make herself feel a tiny smidgen better and kiss the furious look from Joe's face.

No! Madness.

Except he seemed to sense her wildly inappropriate thoughts. His gaze dropped to her lips. He inhaled sharply. His eyes landed back on hers, their dark depths now glowing with intensity and maybe even the barest hint of challenge, as if he too had felt the same illicit urge.

It happened too quickly to analyse. Darcy sensed movement on Joe's part, but she'd already acted on the insane impulse and actually kissed him, her heart rate galloping so high that she grew dizzy.

For a coherent moment of doubt she gasped against his lips, her eyes searching his, but Joe's fingers were curled around her upper arms and showing no sign of letting go. He kissed her back, those strong, capable hands holding her like a vice, his blazing eyes locked to hers as if he too would make some sense of this risky, ill-judged act neither of them seemed able to resist.

He was party to the same madness that had accosted her. Contagious madness that came from being sleep-deprived.

But Darcy was too far gone to consider the fallout of kissing her boss. Her lips tingled where they were crushed against his, darts of electricity firing through every nerve. For the first time today, she felt like herself: strong, capable, determined.

For a heady moment with his mouth on hers, her choppy breaths mingling with his rough exhalations, all the blood in her body pooling in her pelvis, she soared. Every deep-rooted doubt planted in the fertile soil of her insecurities dropped away, lighter than feathers, and she surrendered to pure sensation.

Joe's kiss was firm, commanding and inflamed, and it carried a whiff of desperation, as if he'd thought about kissing her long before this moment of joint insanity. As if he hadn't kissed a woman in a while and the desire was bottled up inside him like oxygen compressed inside a cylinder.

The thought of her hot, divorced boss's sex life made her entire body shudder against his chest. But Darcy hadn't thrown caution to the wind, perhaps even thrown away her glowing reference, in order to swoon at her master's touch.

Owning the kiss, she slid her hands from his broad shoulders, where hard muscles bunched under her palms, and tangled her fingers in his hair, directing his head and touching her tongue to his. He grunted out some unintelligible but sexy sound to which Darcy was deaf. All she could hear was the urgent whoosh of blood through her ears. All she could feel was the exhilaration of the endorphins lacing that blood, the high of kissing Joe a fantasy she realised belatedly she'd secretly harboured since she'd witnessed his first unimpressed sneer.

Joe might not respect her professionally but he seemed equally powerless to their ill-judged attraction.

The reminder that they were colleagues and at work elbowed its way to the forefront of her mind. He was her boss. A man she could grow to loathe if he continued to make her job as difficult as he'd made her first day.

She needed to stop this insanity. Now.

With worrying reluctance, she abandoned his hair and positioned her hands to push at his shoulders, even as her lips clung to his in the dying threads of their reckless and forbidden lip-lock.

In that second her pager emitted an eardrum-shattering bleep. Darcy snatched her mouth away, simultaneously shoving at Joe and jerking to her feet. His hands left her waist with almost unwilling slowness. Confused and disoriented, Darcy looked up from silencing the pager clipped to the waistband of her scrubs.

Joe had retreated behind his scowl once more.

Darcy swallowed, trying to ignore the demands of her libido and quash her disappointment, while trying to appear as unaffected as Joe. They were right back where they'd begun. She'd risked her career for nothing.

'If I still have a job,' she said huskily while she willed the colour in her face to fade, 'I'm needed in A&E.' She tightened her haphazard ponytail, avoiding looking at a gloriously dishevelled Joe—messed hair, dilated pupils, bruised mouth.

He raked his hand over his face, where his stubble darkened his strong jaw, his stare somewhere between bewildered and displeased, and gave her a single curt nod.

'Do you need me?' He stood, his voice gruff and his body rigid, as if trying to claw back a shred of their proper professional relationship. Or perhaps already preparing his dismissal speech.

Who knew what would happen in the cold light of a regular work day? Surely she'd be fired for her outspoken attack and for crossing the line and kissing City Hospital's golden boy.

Darcy touched her mouth. Her cheeks tingled from his stubble, a reminder of the most self-destructive thing she'd ever done. 'Um… I'll let you know.'

What she needed was distance. A chance to analyse what the hell she thought she was doing first arguing with and then kissing her consultant and why she still hadn't outgrown that urge to push herself, be the best she could be, to stand out.

Now look where it had landed her.

She made her way to the emergency department with a sinking stomach as glints of brilliant orange pierced the windows, heralding the dawn of a new day. Too bad it was too late for first impressions.

CHAPTER FIVE

THE FOLLOWING WEEK Joe entered the theatre scrub room, the memory of that kiss thrumming as fresh as if they were still lip-locked. His feet skidded to a halt. He'd been expecting Darcy, of course. He'd requested her assistance in today's complex surgery.

He'd even expected the same euphoric thrill he'd experienced with his mouth on hers—the first woman he'd kissed since his divorce—before his remorse killed the high like a vile-tasting antidote to a sweet, addictive poison.

The door swung closed at his back. Darcy twirled to face him, that now familiar flash of confusion, bravado and need bright in her ocean-blue eyes. He hadn't meant to upset her that night, but he'd seen that look a lot since the kiss—every time they interacted on the ward, in clinic or in Theatre.

'Darcy,' he said in greeting, his voice a grunt strangled by his guilt. Not for the kiss, which while totally unprofessional, he couldn't bring himself to regret, but for bringing his emotional hang-ups into the workplace and making her defensive. To her credit, she hadn't reported him to management for his inappropriate behaviour. She'd merely navigated her job with the same thorough persistence he'd learned was her default position.

But it had left him with more questions than answers.

She'd chosen her career over her fiancé. Why couldn't she have both?

She had regrets. Was that the reason she pushed herself so hard, as he'd once done?

She'd been underestimated, even dismissed in the past, perhaps the reason for the self-doubts she'd confessed. But couldn't she see how exceptional she was?

'Joe,' she said, acting as if everything was normal between them, but up close her eyes were bright with those emotions she'd been trying to conceal all week. Her face was flushed, perhaps with embarrassment, and those delectable lips he recalled the taste of were pursed in defiance. The reminder smacked him in the head with the same force he'd felt when she was crushed against his chest.

But for the shocking intrusion of her pager blaring through the charged atmosphere of the theatre coffee room, she might still be there, captive to the desire she'd awoken in him.

'Thanks for coming to assist.' Joe offered Darcy a tight smile as if they were strangers. He should have apologised sooner, dispelled some of this awkwardness.

'Of course. Where else would I be?' she said, acting with forthright professionalism, when he wanted some answers now that they finally had five minutes alone.

Darcy tied her surgical hat in place. It forced her breasts up and out in his direction, and he had to consciously tear his eyes from the blood-stirring sight she made, his heart slamming against his ribs. He reached for his own surgical hat to stop himself from tucking away that stubborn strand of her blonde hair that always escaped her hat. Now he knew its softness, the faint scent of some sort of floral shampoo, the tickle of it against his face, his fingers burned to touch.

But he had no right. She was his trainee. He'd kissed her like a man starved, tasting her, consuming her throaty little whimpers, learning what made her tremble.

But why had she kissed him back?

Rampant curiosity goaded, made a mockery of his attempts to stay professional.

'Have you performed a Whipple procedure before?' he asked, trying and failing to project a normal tone. Hell, all he wanted to do was kiss her again. Perhaps then he could figure out why those few blissful seconds they'd shared had silenced even his darkest, most intrusive self-recriminatory thoughts.

'Not single-handed.' She cast him a wary look as she tied her mask in place over her beautiful but distracting mouth. 'I've assisted in a handful of cases though, so I'm glad you asked me to help.' She looked away, blinking rapidly.

She clearly wanted to forget the kiss, otherwise she'd have brought it up—Darcy wasn't shy in pushing her agenda or broaching the difficult topics. Perhaps she simply wanted to return to a professional footing. Exactly what he should want.

Except, if forced to admit his deepest darkest desires, he'd need to acknowledge that he wanted Darcy Wright the way he hadn't wanted anyone since his life imploded. A huge part of him was in no way sorry that he'd learned the soft taste of her sensual mouth or the warm feminine scent of her close up or the arousing crush of her breasts against his chest.

Three years without sex was clearly detrimental to his decision-making processes.

But they still needed to work together. It was his job to clear the air. He tied a mask over his mouth to stop any wayward and unprofessional confessions.

'Before we start the surgery, I'd like to apologise.' It was long overdue, his only excuse that he'd tried to maintain some sort of distance over the intervening days, as if to raise the subject of what happened that night would force him to admit the rush he'd experienced when that long-dormant part of him had roared alive at her touch. He'd been Frankenstein's monster reawakened—still cobbled together pieces of his former self, but surprised to find that his bruised and battered heart still functioned.

'I made your first day…difficult.' He winced. 'It's no excuse, but I was going through some… personal stuff. I want you to know that it wasn't my intention to upset you when I mentioned your CV, which, by the way, is very impressive.'

For a second she stared. He braced himself for the inevitable questions or contradictions. 'Thank you.' Then she stepped up to the stainless steel sink and switched on the taps. 'So, I've reviewed the scans and I can see why this case is so complex.' She continued their prior conversation as if he hadn't changed the subject.

What? Where was the tongue-lashing he deserved? Why wasn't she putting him in his place? Unease slithered down his spine—she did seem a little subdued today.

'Darcy,' he said, his tone serious.

She glanced his way and their eyes locked, the connection instant and exaggerated now that they knew the taste of each other. Joe almost forgot himself and where he was, almost reached out and touched her.

'We need to discuss what happened.' He needed to dissect it and then put it to rest. Then he needed to keep his eyes, hands and lips to himself. Joe started the taps next to hers, doused his hands and arms in the warm water.

Perhaps she'd be more amenable to hearing him out while they prepared for surgery.

Joe reached for a single use scrubbing brush from the dispenser. Darcy reached for one at the same time. Their arms collided. Their hands tangled.

Darcy yanked her arm away as if she'd been scalded.

'After you,' said Joe, breathing through the jolt of heat incinerating his body.

Kissing her that night should have brought him to his senses, shocked his system back into the soul-draining numbness he'd inhabited for the past four years, the place he preferred because that was where he felt closest to Rosie. Only Darcy plagued his every non-work-related thought. Not just the kiss, which was unforgettable enough and fodder for some pretty erotic dreams, from which he woke sweating and hard, but also the flashes of vulnerability she'd shown him that day.

She snatched a packet from the dispenser and tore into it. 'I guess the fact that we're still on first name basis and you haven't fired me yet means we can't avoid this conversation any longer.'

'Why would I fire you?'

She flicked her stare his way, her eyes sincere above her mask. 'Because I shouldn't have done…what I did on call. I was obviously stressed and exhausted. So I'd like to apologise, too. For…you know…the kiss.' She attacked her forearms with the scrubber, the suds stained yellow from the iodine.

Wait… She was taking responsibility for the kiss? Had she missed the way he'd fixated on her mouth, his brain foggy and distracted by the apparent softness of those full lips? Had she forgotten the way he'd crushed her to him like a drowning man, the way that even after the violent and unwelcome intrusion of her pager he'd struggled to relinquish his hold?

For something to do other than yank her back into his arms, Joe began the second-nature ritual of scrubbing up, leaving his mind free to fill in the blanks. Had she needed the balm of his lips as much as he'd needed to taste hers? Something primal shifted inside him. He got to her. It seemed only fair—she'd been under his skin since the moment they'd met on the ward.

'I'm your boss. I crossed a line, Darcy.' Not that he'd change a thing about the kiss itself.

He looked over at her stilled form. He could tell from the look in her eyes that her mask concealed an astonished expression. 'No, *I* crossed the line.'

Joe grinned behind his mask. Typical that Darcy needed to win the pointless argument of who'd made the first move when the real issue was ensuring that it never happened again.

But now she'd given his curiosity an open door.

'And why exactly did you do that?' Joe's nervous system sparked alive. It shouldn't matter why, only he was having a hard time stopping himself from peeling down her mask and repeating the error, God help him.

Darcy's eyes went wide with a flicker of fear, gone as soon as it appeared. She scrubbed at her hands hard enough to leave red welts behind. 'I don't know…'

'Liar.' He stepped closer, his stare laser-focused on hers, water and suds dripping down his arms and onto the floor at their feet. 'Don't forget that I felt your heart thunder and your breath gust. I heard the throaty little moans you couldn't hold inside.'

Why was he pursuing this, goading her to admit something that was irrelevant? Was he a glutton for punishment? Or simply already addicted to the feeling of being alive, to the transient amnesia he suffered around Darcy?

She sluiced her arms under the water, feigning indifference. 'Perhaps I was frustrated that my first day had been a battleground. Perhaps it was payback for how you rattled my confidence with your…hovering. Or maybe it was just plain old temporary insanity.' Abandoning her composure, she whirled to face him, her eyes ablaze. 'Take your pick.' She reached for her mask and tugged it down.

'No, no, no.' His voice was a seductive growl he barely recognised. 'Temporary insanity is *my* excuse.'

Except he'd known exactly what he was doing. She'd awoken him from an emotional drought with her sass and grit, evoking a rampant desire to know if her lips would taste as good as they looked.

They had. Better, in fact. And he hadn't wanted to stop.

'Another thing we have in common then,' she said, with a tremulous quality to her normally clear voice that heated Joe's blood.

'Perhaps…' Lust punched him below the waist as she looked up at him with widened pupils. 'But

I don't routinely go around kissing my registrars; in fact, I haven't kissed anyone since my divorce.'

Joe inched closer. 'I've never met a woman so…provoking.' His eyes strayed repeatedly to her mouth, the urge to kiss her again so intense he almost forgot that he'd spent the past five minutes rendering his hands and arms sterile for the impending surgery. Because with their stares locked, and her lips parted, he was struggling to care.

'So why kiss me?' Her chest moved with her rapid breaths.

'Perhaps I hoped that tasting your lips would shunt me back to normal, knock the sense back into me.'

Only it had backfired. Her lips had been soft and desperate, her soft moan barely audible but resonating so deeply with his own desperation and need he'd had to curl his fingers around a handful of her scrub top to stop himself from uttering the feral growl trapped in his throat.

For endless seconds they stood facing each other, too close for colleagues, wet arms and blazing stares the only barrier to everything Joe wanted to say and know and do. The patient wasn't in the operating theatre yet. For one unthinkable second he fantasised about reigniting the madness that had clearly infected them both that night. Every cell in his body felt the urge to pull down his own mask and take her mouth, lose himself until she looked at him the way she had in the on-call staffroom, just before that kiss.

She hadn't been able to stop herself from kissing Joe the man, and he'd been whole for a few minutes, not the damaged animal he'd been every day for the past four long years.

But Joe was that broken man and all the other complex permutations of himself to boot.

'So, what now?' she asked, her voice a whisper, her eyes searching. The newly awakened man in him wanted to see the same wild desperation he'd witnessed when she'd dragged her wet mouth from his, her lips swollen from his desire. It was there in the background, but there was also what looked like understanding, compassion.

That he didn't need.

Joe reined in his urgent and highly inappropriate thoughts, fresh regret dragging at his limbs as he turned back to the sinks. 'Now we perform this Whipple together. I need your help.'

Darcy stood frozen for a few seconds and then nodded with resignation, her long lashes fluttering as she glanced down at the floor. 'Of course.'

Joe resumed scrubbing his hands. Earlier he'd put Darcy's sudden reserve down to embarrassment or lingering resentment for the way he'd treated her that first day. But what if her change in demeanour these past few days meant something else?

With a blow that winded him somewhere in his midsection Joe connected the dots. Her shift in attitude wasn't fear for her job or awkwardness following the kiss.

It was pity.

She knew. About Rosie and how the man she'd wanted that night was a shell—cracked, shattered.

'You know, don't you? About my daughter.' With fiery shame in his veins, he scrubbed his forearms with over-enthusiastic vigour until his skin turned red. 'You've availed yourself of the hospital gossip network.' He couldn't have kept his past a secret for ever, but he'd have preferred that she hear the truth from him direct.

She had the decency to flush, but Joe couldn't bear to see the sympathy in her eyes. He wanted to forget again, to have her look at him the way she had when she'd been in his arms, her breath mingling with his, her fingers tangling and tugging his hair. She kissed like she operated, like she fought her corner. With determination and assertiveness that had somehow roused the man in him from a soulless four-year slumber.

Of course, he was gossip fodder at City Hospital. Even before they'd lost Rosie, his surgical renown and Laura's public persona had created a stir when he'd first arrived, giving him minor celebrity status he'd always dismissed. But did she also know the sordid details of his inadequacies and deepest regrets? How the mighty Joe Austin had once had it all, taken it for granted, been too busy caring for others to notice the seriousness of his own daughter's undiagnosed condition?

'I… I'm sorry.' Darcy dragged him from reliving his pain. 'I promise you I wasn't prying or gossiping.'

Joe couldn't bring himself to look at her again, his unfocused stare aimed at the suds swirling in the sink.

'Some of the surgical staff mentioned the open invitation to your garden party on Saturday and…'

Joe ignored her reasonable tone, brushed aside the fact that he'd meant to issue the invitation to her himself. 'And you discovered that it's in memory of Rosie. Is that why you've been avoiding me? Why you stopped pushing on every patient management decision we've made this week? Out of pity for the broken man who was desperate to forget his grief for a few seconds and kissed you?'

The scrubbing brush dug into the sensitive skin under his fingernails and he welcomed the pain. Perhaps it would act like acupuncture, the physical sting overwhelming the emotional.

'Don't be ridiculous.' Her fire returned. 'Empathy for your loss isn't pity, Joe.' She braced her hands on the edge of the sink as if collecting herself and then pinned him with her determined gaze. 'I'm a doctor; caring for other human beings comes naturally. And I'll always push my own agenda. That's who I am.'

Until now, that facet of her complex personality had earned his fascination and respect.

'Of course you will.' He'd never met anyone with more to prove than Darcy. 'Well, don't worry—your efforts haven't been in vain. I've noticed your dedication this past week—you're on the ward before me every day, leave after me every night, which, considering that I practically live here, is impressive bordering on sycophantic.'

Outrage returned to her glare. 'I'm not sucking up to you. It's my job, a job I love, and I want to be good at it.' She looked deflated and Joe glimpsed that vulnerability once more, his heart thumping with gratitude that he wasn't alone.

She glanced up. 'I need to be good at it.'

Joe frowned. Why? And why would she confess such a thing, to him of all people? To her he was a demanding, unreasonable boss at best and a sad grief-stricken divorcee at worst. But it was all irrelevant. He'd been carried away by that addictive mental silence when he'd kissed her, consumed by feeling normal, like a red-blooded man, indulging again, when all she felt for him was sympathy.

'Listen,' Darcy said, interrupting his reverie, 'I won't come on Saturday if it would be…inappropriate.'

Oh, no, he couldn't leave things this way. They faced a complicated procedure this afternoon, so he needed to wrap up this disastrous conversation. But he *was* a red-blooded man. He was broken, yes, but he wasn't dead. If he focused on their attraction, one he knew she reciprocated, perhaps he could distract himself from the self-loathing he felt at any mention of Rosie's name, and distract Darcy until she looked at him like she needed the connection, the life-affirming thrill as much as he did. Indulging his attraction was risky; he was her boss. But he could detach his feelings from the workplace. Darcy would soon move on and he'd never allow his attraction to influence her career.

He smiled, the expression brittle. 'You're very welcome—I'd planned to invite you anyway. The weather is forecast to be glorious, the food will be delicious and it will be a great opportunity for you to socialise with the rest of the surgical staff.' He rinsed the iodine-coloured suds from his arms and turned off the taps with his elbows, holding his wet arms up between them. 'But by all means stay away if our obvious attraction will make you uncomfortable.'

She swallowed, her inhale shuddering through her as she tried to grapple control over her body.

'As for the kiss…' He slowly traced her parted lips with his stare. 'I would apologise, too, only I just can't bring myself to regret it.'

He moved to the swing door to the operating room, casting her a final pointed look. 'But for your pager going off, I might not have stopped. Think on that next time you feel sorry for me.'

The desire that lit her eyes momentarily pierced the shock on her face, but it was little comfort. For now, she'd infected his blood and no amount of scrubbing could eradicate the truth. He wanted to be immune to the way she made him feel. Now that she saw him for who he was, knew all his sordid little secrets, he *needed* to be immune. And, like any disease, there was only one way to build up that resilience, to remove Darcy from his system so he could again feel normal: greater exposure.

CHAPTER SIX

DARCY NIBBLED AT her lip and glanced around the immaculate garden of the family home in the Surrey countryside just outside London. Joe was nowhere to be seen. A stitch settled under her ribs and the delicious mouthful of Pimm's and lemonade soured on her tongue as her gaze swept over the back of the house and the open French windows. She couldn't seem to stop her almost frantic search.

Just one glimpse of him; that was all she wanted. So she'd know he was okay, surviving this difficult day and all its memories.

She thought back to the day of the Whipple surgery, the stomach-churning mix of desire and doubt. No one liked to think they were the source of local gossip, but why was Joe so defensive about his daughter's death? The tragedy of losing his little girl, while devastating, wasn't his fault.

Unless he blamed himself somehow.

At least his personal experience explained his caution and conscientiousness.

She'd tried to stay away from today's event, to show him that the last thing she felt was pity, that the last thing she wanted to do was pry into his still raw grief, but his words had swirled through her mind, drawing her to him like a constant lure.

As for the kiss... I just can't bring myself to regret it.

Neither could she. Her stomach swooped, all nervous anticipation and fizzing excitement. Surely he'd make an appearance soon.

'Beautiful, isn't it?' said Isha, who had one eye on her energetic daughter. Together with a rag-tag group of other children of varying ages, the sweet ten-year-old with her mother's eyes was trying to negotiate the rules for the croquet set up on the pristine lawn.

Darcy nodded, fussing with the frilly neckline of her prettiest sundress. She'd spent way too long preparing for this event, gone all out with subtle make-up and products designed to transform her poker-straight hair into a careless, textured style as if she'd spent the day at the beach. Perhaps Joe had been and left and wouldn't even witness her efforts to look good. For him.

'I'm not sure I should have come,' said Darcy, nerves jittering in her chest. 'I feel like an imposter.' Especially after her last real conversation with Joe unrelated to work had ended in confusion and renewed wariness. 'He doesn't even like me and I'm standing on his lawn sipping Pimm's.'

This was a mistake. But after the shock of discovering that Joe had lost his only child, she'd needed to reassure herself, to witness his resilience and to be there if he needed…

What? She snorted. If he needed to talk he wouldn't seek out Darcy. Their current communication style was formal and polite, to say the least.

'Don't be ridiculous,' Isha said. She'd been the one to encourage Darcy to attend the garden party, which, together with the infamous Christmas party fund-raiser, seemed to be the talked-about surgical department social event of the year. 'He's asked about you every day this week.' Isha took a sip of her drink and waved hello across the garden at a striking, heavily pregnant brunette who looked vaguely familiar.

Darcy practically cricked her neck with the speed she swivelled to stare, gobsmacked, at Isha. 'He has not.' Treacherous fingers of delight danced down Darcy's spine. She hadn't been able to stop thinking about Joe; had he been similarly preoccupied?

Had he scoured the hospital for a chance glance of her? Had he awoken from hot, sweaty dreams where the unwelcome interruption of that call to A&E had never happened?

The nurse nodded slowly, a knowing grin compressing her lips. ‘He has. But don’t worry. He’s careful to ask under the guise of checking that you’ve settled at City. But he can’t fool me.’ Isha tapped the side of her nose and winked. ‘I’ve seen the way he looks at you when he thinks no one is watching.’

‘Oh, stop. He’s my boss.’ Darcy hid her conflicted euphoria behind an exaggerated roll of her eyes. She was the one who needed reminding that Joe was strictly off-limits. She jammed her sunglasses back on her face and looked away to where Isha’s husband was discussing football with a few theatre staff and nurses she recognised.

‘Don’t believe me, huh…’ said Isha. ‘Well, how do you explain that he never asked about your predecessor’s well-being? Not once in six months. Whereas with you he seems to require a daily update.’

Just like she sought him out at every opportunity. Oh, she was careful to disguise her obsession—seeking his medical advice or updating him on a particular patient. But perhaps she was fooling only herself.

Despite her sternest internal lecture to discount as preposterous the information Isha had just shared, elation sang through her bloodstream, making her hot and restless and even more desperate to see Joe.

The unfinished business between them was stacked sky-high.

Darcy bit into a chunk of ice, the well-timed frigid shock the jolt she needed. What was she thinking? She was his registrar—they couldn't happen. Only they kind of already had—that kiss, their botched apologies, his startling and extremely hot confession that he was as into that kiss as she'd been.

Darcy fanned her face and stepped further into the shade of a giant oak tree in the centre of the lawn. 'That's because he's a control freak who doesn't trust me to order an X-ray without his say-so.'

She winced at her disloyalty. He was *her* control freak.

Now she knew that he'd lost his daughter she understood that he had good reason. She couldn't blame him for being thorough, overly cautious, meticulous. Doctors set higher standards for themselves when it came to the health of their loved ones, probably the reason they weren't allowed to treat family members—too close, too emotional, no perspective.

Which also accurately described her Joe-seeking behaviour today.

She scanned the party once more, eyes burning for sight of him, fingers tingling to touch him the way she almost had in the scrub room the other day. Darcy swallowed the anticipation lodged in her tight throat. Despite Isha's insinuation, anything beyond the wary tension they currently shared seemed insurmountable.

She needed to confront him again, outside of the hospital. To work out this mess away from the expectations of their professional roles, where they could just be Joe and Darcy, a man and a woman having an honest conversation about how to navigate their undeniable attraction.

Recognising the direction of her thoughts, she swallowed hard. What was she thinking?

Darcy's priority had to be her career. She'd abandoned the small gains and big losses of dating to climb this final slope to the pinnacle, her consultant job. She couldn't risk it all for a… fling, no matter how tempting.

Fortunately, Joe was too professional to put them in that position. He hadn't dated since his divorce. Despite returning that kiss she'd smacked on him, he'd given no sign he intended to allow this to go any further. Like Darcy, he valued his job. And besides…everything she did seemed to provoke him.

This mounting evidence to support her decision should reassure, only she felt…deflated.

'It looks to me that you're equally invested in

his whereabouts,' said Isha with a smidgen of sympathy in her perceptive eyes. 'You haven't stopped searching him out since we arrived.'

Darcy glanced down at the ground, pretending to examine the heel of her sandal. She needed to be more careful if her growing infatuation was that obvious.

All week she'd tried to focus on work, on their patients and the million jobs in a standard day in the life of a surgical registrar, but respect for the man she was desperately trying to ignore had become overwhelming. He spoke to the patients with a compassion and honesty she tried to emulate. He knew them as well as she did—every blood result and X-ray finding, the names of their loved ones and favourite pastimes.

'I want to know that he's okay with my being here, that's all.' And that caring part of her needed to be on hand to offer comfort. She couldn't even fathom what it must be like to lose a child.

Just then Isha's husband called her over. Darcy smiled and wandered over towards a stunning wilderness area alive with bees dancing between every type of flower.

'Darcy…that is you?' a male voice said.

Darcy looked up, her disappointment that the man addressing her wasn't the one she wanted to see locked behind a polite smile.

'Aaron—what are you doing here?' She shook

his hand and he pulled her close for one of those awkward hug and cheek-kiss combinations of people who came from the same place but only really knew each other in passing.

'I heard you'd taken a job at City. I'm tutoring the newest intake of general practitioners there this term.'

Darcy, nodded, a stab of homesickness catching her by surprise. Aaron was a rural GP from Abbotsford, Darcy's home town. 'Look out for Stella. She's on the GP training programme, so she might be in one of your lectures.'

At the mention of her sister's name, his smile seemed strained, his expression shifty. 'I will…'

Darcy's curiosity flared. Stella had a bit of a crush on Aaron years ago. Could there be something going on between them…? She'd have to push her sister for details later.

'So, you're working for Joe?' said Aaron, collecting himself.

Darcy nodded, her pulse picking up at the opportunity to talk about the man never far from her thoughts. 'How do you two know each other?'

'We met at med school, flatted together for a couple of years, back in the old days.' Aaron looked across the garden with a fond smile, 'Molly and I were friends with Joe and Laura before…well…you know.'

Before Aaron's wife Molly died, leaving him

a single parent to their newborn baby—the story was the local tragedy back home—and before Joe and Laura divorced.

'She looks great,' Aaron continued, his gaze focused on the gorgeous pregnant brunette. 'I'm happy for her. If only Joe could move on, too.'

Darcy followed his line of sight to Joe's ex-wife, who Darcy guessed was in her third trimester. 'That's Laura Knight?' Of course Joe's ex would be here.

Aaron nodded. 'Have you met her?'

Reeling, Darcy shook her head. Before she could acknowledge the inappropriate rush of possession she felt for Joe, her breath trapped in her lungs. Joe chose that moment to appear from the back of the house and join his ex and the tall greying man with his hand in the small of her back, who was presumably the bump's father.

Blind to the others in the group, Darcy's eyes stung at the sight of Joe dressed casually in faded jeans and navy T-shirt. Still heart-stoppingly gorgeous, he looked…different. The relaxed outfit somehow softened him, made him more complexly human, more three-dimensional and real. It was as if the ex-husband and father elements of him amplified outside of the hospital environment. Here, in his former back garden, he seemed like just a man. A virile, steadfast, reliable and honourable man, who was nonetheless driven by demons, loss and grief.

Darcy's heart clenched violently. Why did that call to her on so many levels? Why couldn't she keep Joe Austin and all his niggling negatives at arm's length emotionally? Was it just her doctor's gene, a reflex need to help people in pain? Or was it the fact that, professionally, since the Whipple operation, she felt that he needed her, trusted her a little more?

Darcy gulped her drink to hide the glut of confusing feelings from Joe's friend.

Just then Joe glanced in their direction. His eyes locked with Darcy's and her body actually shuddered. The warm summer-scented air stilled. The hum of insects and the chatter of surrounding conversations dimmed.

Stripped bare, Darcy wondered if all of the assembled guests, Joe included, could see every one of her emotions.

They hadn't been alone since the Whipple operation. Since they'd acknowledged the kiss—Darcy with an apology and Joe with his stark admission that he hadn't wanted it to stop. And they weren't alone now, but they might as well be for the heat and awareness that connected his stare to hers as if by an invisible thread that stretched across the lawn.

All of the reasons they couldn't be that she'd cemented in her mind crumbled.

He wanted her. She wanted him—he was gorgeous, and that single half-arsed kiss had blown her mind. Darcy felt as if she might actually melt into a puddle. Her body came alive, her breasts tingled and heat pooled between her legs.

Joe pressed a kiss to his ex-wife's cheek, shook her new partner's hand and then made a beeline for her and Aaron. Every relaxed step he took across the grass jolted through Darcy's weakened body like a shockwave. When his stare swooped from her eyes to her chest, and lower, she felt it caress her skin as sure as if it were his warm, confident touch.

Darcy swallowed past her dry throat. She was in so much trouble.

While Joe and Aaron exchanged warm greetings with mutual back slaps and genuine laughter, Darcy contemplated running away. She'd done what she'd come here to do: ensure he was okay. Except it made her breath catch to see Joe's face transformed during the moment of unguarded joy as he welcomed his friend. How was it possible for him to be any hotter, and why was she so desperate to be the reason for his happy, relaxed smile?

'Darcy, thanks for coming along.' His voice carried none of the anger and accusation of their last personal conversation, only warmth and something else, something exhilarating that sounded like a secret code. He kept his hands to himself, to Darcy's relief. If he'd touched her or politely kissed her cheek in her current conflicted state, she might actually hurl herself into his arms in front of all assembled.

'You were right about the weather,' she said in a panicked search for appropriate words. 'What a beautiful day.' She chewed the inside of her cheek, disgusted that, after waiting so long for him to appear, her concern growing with every second, all she could dredge up was an observation on the weather, when she had so much to say, to ask, to understand and explore.

She searched Joe's eyes for his feelings. Should she offer words of condolence? Would he want her sympathy when things between them were so…complicated and strained? She hated that he thought she pitied him, when the opposite was closer to the truth. In the face of his loss, she respected him even more for being the man she'd come to know: kind, dedicated, sexy as hell…

'I'll leave you two to catch up,' croaked Darcy, shuffling away from the friends when all she wanted to do was get Joe alone. But this wasn't the time or place and being alone with him was… dangerous.

At least she'd seen with her own eyes that he seemed fine.

Joe's hand landed on her arm, halting her escape. 'Can you spare me a minute?'

She froze under his touch, which was warm and electric and way too tempting to deny. Aaron muttered something about refilling his drink and sauntered casually away.

Finally alone, Darcy faced Joe, tongue-tied for the first time in her life.

'It's good to see you away from work.' His stare was banked with sincerity, searching and intense. The force of it, the way heat burned across her skin confirmed that at least to her body Joe was primarily a man, not her boss.

He stepped infinitesimally closer, the way Darcy longed to do, but her feet were stuck on the grass, her knees so wobbly she'd had to lock them to stay upright. 'We need to talk—I've been…thinking.'

Yes, her too! Only now he stood before her in the flesh, his dark hair lifted by the breeze, his haunted eyes narrowed against the sun and his familiar scent bathing her in a delicious cloud, she had the strong urge to hide from his extreme magnetism and her convoluted feelings.

'I know this must be a very difficult day for you.' *Don't touch him. Don't touch him.* 'I'm so sorry, Joe.'

His sadness-touched smile was unadorned. 'No more difficult than every other day.'

Darcy's heart cracked for him. The gift of his honesty and openness pulsed through her until she was certain she'd act on the compulsion to hold him. He flashed the guarded smile he usually wore at a group not far from them, reminding Darcy that while she might feel as if they were the only two people who existed, they were no more alone than at the hospital.

Would she need to wait for their next night on call to get him to herself? Except she wanted, no, needed, all the barriers she could find. They kept her on course, reminded her why she was single. Because sometimes, like now, when she caught Joe's eye, momentarily forgot he was her boss, she questioned her choice.

But that was just lust.

'What were you thinking?' Could those around them see her body's desire for him? Could they tell, even as she clung to her denial, that if she wasn't careful she'd have to acknowledge other feelings, alarming feelings?

No—it was just professional respect.

Joe winced, his expression torn. 'Now isn't really the time.' He glanced back at his ex-wife, who smiled. Darcy sensed their ongoing connection and shuffled her feet, unsettled. What must it be like to lose a child? How did Joe feel, seeing his ex move on? Were they still as close as they seemed, and why should it matter so much to Darcy, who neither wanted nor had any claim?

'Can we meet for a coffee, outside of work?' he said, sending her pulse galloping. 'Are you free tomorrow?'

The strength to make an excuse drained away. 'Okay…' Her voice was an anxious croak, as well it should be. Meeting away from the hospital sent a certain message. They weren't friends. Would it be a date? Would he suggest a wild sex-only fling so they could get all of this tension out of their systems? Would she run for safety or leap into his arms, lips first?

Just then a cry startled them both from their bubble of intimacy. Darcy's eyes flew to the source of the sound, her adrenaline soaring to high alert.

She heard Joe's gasp at the same moment he grabbed for her hand, as if acting on instinct. He jerked into action, taking Darcy along too.

Hand in hand, as if it was the most natural thing in the world, they raced across the lawn towards what was clearly some sort of emergency. Darcy's drink spilled over her free hand before her brain kicked in and she passed the glass to a startled guest.

Joe and Darcy skidded to a halt at the small huddle of horrified adults. The child at the centre was no more than eight years old and lay, pale and lifeless, on the grass. Flecks of bright green pond weed clung to her hair, making her pallid skin even more waxen.

Darcy dropped to her knees on the other side of the little girl. Joe leaned over the girl's head, checked for signs of breath on his cheek. Darcy fingered her tiny wrist and then her neck for a pulse.

Their eyes locked over the girl's lifeless form. Darcy nodded and Joe shook his head, silent communication loud and clear between them. She had a pulse but wasn't breathing.

'What happened?' asked Joe as he rolled the child onto her side to clear the water from her mouth.

'She was running,' said the mother with imploring eyes. 'She tripped and fell into the pond. I think she must have hit her head because she can swim, but she didn't. Please help her.'

Joe rolled the girl onto her back and inflated her chest with a rescue breath. 'Can you still feel a pulse?' he asked Darcy.

'Yes, but it's faint,' said Darcy, focused on Joe and the girl. 'Could be a concussion.' She quickly examined the girl's head and found a scalp contusion under her hairline. 'Looks like she did bump her head, perhaps on one of the rocks.'

Joe nodded and continued resuscitation, his

calm determination a wondrous sight in the highly emotive atmosphere.

Darcy took command of the surrounding situation, recruiting Aaron to herd the guests inside the house and give them space. Every face was etched with distress and they didn't need an audience.

'Does she have any health conditions?' Darcy spoke to the child's parents, gleaning her medical history, while Joe breathed for her. 'Is she on any medication?'

The frantic parents shook their heads in unison. Darcy felt again for a pulse and gave Joe a reassuring nod.

With that the girl spluttered and coughed up a mouthful of water. Joe turned her onto her side and placed her in the recovery position, elation bright in his eyes. Eyes that clung to Darcy's as if he needed her presence in order to breathe.

Darcy's heart swooped in her chest, her own relief for the little girl, her parents and for Joe a high in her blood. She recalled the way he'd gripped her hand almost instinctively, as if he'd needed her in that moment of surging adrenaline.

Darcy sagged back on her heels. Her feelings for Joe roared out of control. The event had been scary enough for all of them, but for Joe, today of all days, a near miss like that would likely trigger all sorts of sorrow.

Darcy took the blanket someone had retrieved from the house and draped it over the child's slender body.

Joe rested his hand on top of Darcy's on the girl's shoulder. 'Thank you.' He swallowed. His low words were just for her and emotion blazed from his eyes, dragging an answering surge from deep within Darcy's chest. It was as if they were the only two people in the garden again.

Or maybe it was just the adrenaline, pure and simple. It was one thing to tackle medical emergencies at the hospital, but out in the community, without equipment or drugs, another matter entirely.

'*You* revived her,' Darcy said, checking the girl's pupillary reflexes, although she knew from the pink tinge to her skin that she was out of imminent danger.

Her sobbing parents knelt and talked to their daughter, whose name was Holly, soothing her with comforts and reassurances.

'She'll need to go to A and E,' explained Darcy, because Joe had fallen into a pensive silence. 'She'll need to be checked out and she might need a scan to exclude any head injury.'

Darcy wanted to hold Joe so badly; she had to remind herself where and who they were. Just because she felt a greater connection to him, felt as if he truly valued her as a colleague, didn't mean he had any feelings for her as a woman, beyond simple physical attraction.

And she shouldn't have feelings for him either.

When the paramedics arrived Joe and Darcy handed over Holly's care, supplying a succinct history of what had occurred to the ambulance crew.

Once more alone, side by side on the lawn, Darcy sensed Joe's withdrawal, chiding herself for her flight of fancy. Of course, he had no feelings for her. He was grieving. He was the host and, even though it seemed the party was over, he had friends, family, responsibilities here.

Yes, he'd needed her at a time of medical crisis, but life had taught her to never place her vulnerable heart into the hands of another. Ten minutes ago she'd wanted to get away from Joe and the way he made her feel the first tender shoots of romantic possibility.

She should trust that instinct.

CHAPTER SEVEN

JOE'S ENTIRE BODY sagged with relief as his car rounded the bend in the gravel driveway of the house he'd once shared with his wife and daughter. Darcy stood outside the gates under the shade of a tree, her face downturned to her phone. How could just the sight of her in her pretty floral sundress be such a balm, today of all days, especially in light of the close call with little Holly?

Because he couldn't get her out of his mind, that was why.

How had she, this fiery, forthright woman, penetrated the fog he'd lived under for four years, like a lone but warming ray of sun? How had she somehow kick-started a part of him relegated to irrelevant while he'd dealt with his grief over his inadequacies as a father and husband? Not that he was miraculously cured—he'd never be free of his regrets. But perhaps the universe was trying to tell him that he still had worth as a man, not just as a doctor. That he needed more than work.

But did he deserve more?

He pulled up and jumped out of the car. He hadn't realised how much he needed to see the smile in her eyes, albeit hesitant, until he basked in it now.

'I thought you'd left ages ago.' While he'd wrapped up the party and reassured the guests that he, Laura and Holly would be fine. The minute he could reasonably leave he'd snatched up his keys and made a bid for escape, that part of him that had reached for her hand seeking Darcy out among the last party stragglers.

'Isha and her family had to leave,' she said in explanation. 'But I wanted to make sure that Holly and her parents were okay.'

Joe nodded, grateful now, as always, for her compassionate and professional nature. 'Do you need a lift?' He breathed through the rapid thumping of his heart, refusing to acknowledge how much he needed her to say yes.

'I was just going to order a ride.' She waggled her phone in his direction.

Her eyes, those deep pools of blue, saw way too much of his shredded composure. While he prided himself as a guarded and private man, Darcy seemed an expert at peeling back his layers. Was that why he'd reached for her hand the minute the emergency registered in his head? Because he needed her in order to feel…better, to feel something other than the flat, colourless emotional void of his pre-Darcy existence?

'I'm going back to London. I can take you.'

She frowned and he shoved his hands into his pockets.

'I'm trying to get you alone, Darcy, for that talk we discussed earlier.' And because she filled his head morning and night and something had to be done. Should he find her another position, out of temptation's way? A surgical registrar of Darcy's calibre would be an asset to any team. She'd be snapped up. He'd come to depend on her, handing over more and more responsibility this week while he'd left work at a reasonable hour in order to assist Laura with the preparations for today's fundraiser.

More importantly, though, the thought of not seeing her every day left him hollow and restless.

Joe opened the passenger door and shot her his *I mean business* look. 'Just get in so we can get out of here—it's been a long day.'

'Okay, sure. Thanks,' she said, her smile wobbling as if with nerves. Without further argument, she slid into the passenger seat and buckled her seat belt.

Joe climbed in and set off. For a long time they sat in loaded silence, as if neither of them wanted to break the tension that filled the car. Joe wound through the country lanes, his focus on the road but his awareness of Darcy breathing next to him, her light floral scent rousing his senses, made him grip the steering wheel tighter in case his hands decided to tremble. In case he pulled the car into the nearest lane and dragged her to his kiss.

'I called the hospital and spoke to Holly's mum,' said Darcy, her tone soft and reassuring, the way he'd heard her speak to distraught relatives or seriously ill patients. 'They're keeping her in overnight for observation, but the CT scan was all clear.'

'That's good.' Joe hid the mess of his conflicted emotions behind a tight smile.

'She was lucky that it happened in your garden,' she said, respect clear in her expression.

Darcy's calm, confident presence had soothed the rage of his pulse and the roar of his adrenaline-laced blood. Not that he'd forgotten his first response training, although it had been a while since he'd managed an emergency outside of the hospital and without a team of other staff. But the seriousness and timing of the incident—a day when his thoughts naturally revolved around Rosie and how she should be there, running around the lawn in her bare feet, dark hair flying behind her—struck him with a wave of fresh grief.

'Or unlucky—I should have drained that pond

years ago,' Joe said pointedly, his regrets returning tenfold.

While focused on providing mouth-to-mouth resuscitation to the child, he'd had to stop himself from imagining it was Rosie whose life he'd been attempting to save. The relief of Holly's first spluttered breath had been overwhelming and disorientating because she was another man's beloved daughter, not his.

Rosie was still gone.

'That's not true, Joe. Accidents happen every day. She tripped and hit her head. That can happen anywhere, and we both know that children can deteriorate quickly, but also recover just as speedily.'

As if realising that recovery wasn't always the case, she sucked in a gasp.

Joe glanced at Darcy. She wore the same expression she'd had when his eyes had sought hers after reviving Holly. Her gaze filled with understanding, as if she knew his innermost thoughts, understood his conflicts and wanted to comfort him.

'Are you okay?' she whispered, conveying their new and growing intimacy.

He swallowed, feeling anything but okay. He wanted so many things in that moment. He wanted Darcy with something close to a terrifying ferocity. Because the way he felt around her confused him, as if she lessened his pain and he'd forgotten how to live without his grief. His grief was his only connection to Rosie. He'd cling to it until his own final breath.

'Define okay?' He focused on navigating the roundabout, when all he wanted to do was touch her face, trace the sun-kissed freckles across her nose, slide his fingers through her hair, drag those lush lips to his until the noise in his head fell silent. He'd tried but he couldn't stop craving the release he'd experienced when they'd kissed that first night. He couldn't switch off his eagerness to know everything about her, not just as a doctor but as a woman, a friend, a sister and daughter...

She sighed, her hand twitching in her lap. He curled his fingers around the steering wheel to stop himself from reaching out to hold that hand once more, because it had felt so good there during those few brief moments.

'Today can't have been easy for you,' she said. 'I guess I'm asking in a not-so-subtle way if you want to talk about it.'

He swallowed, so tempted to lay himself bare to her. Perhaps he'd scare her away and he wouldn't need to deal with his feelings of inconvenient attraction. Normally he avoided talking about Rosie. While he thought about her constantly, discussing his little girl amplified his guilt and failure as a father.

Words couldn't bring her back.

'Not easy on you either, with the unexpected emergency,' he hedged, waiting for the lid on his emotions to snap closed, as it usually did when anyone strayed too far into his personal territory. 'Are *you* okay?'

'I'm fine.' She smiled and something shifted in his chest. 'I was shaken, of course. The adrenaline and the thought of the possible consequences.'

Joe nodded. Darcy was right about how rapidly children, in particular, could deteriorate. Rosie had gone downhill over a few short hours.

They stopped at traffic lights. 'I'm… I'm glad you were there,' he said. This time he did reach for her hand.

'I'm glad you were there, too.' She gripped his fingers the way she'd done as they'd run to help Holly. They both stared at her lap, at their hands entwined there, neither speaking or moving a muscle as if acutely aware of the momentousness of the simple comforting gesture.

The lights changed. He released her hand reluctantly. 'It's been a while since I performed CPR out in the field.' Darcy's junior status meant she'd much more likely have encountered an acute head injury emergency more recently than him. In the few short weeks they'd known each other he'd come to rely on her clinical acumen and clear-headed decisions.

'You were great,' she said.

Their eyes met. They were skating the issue, the big conversation.

'You know I mean it, Joe… If you want to talk, I'm happy to listen. I can only imagine what you and Laura have been through.'

'You met Laura?' Why was the idea of that so strange? Laura was remarried. He respected Phil, her second husband, even liked him. Were his feelings for Darcy, his strengthening obsession, bordering on more than desire…?

No, he couldn't allow that.

She nodded, her stare wary. 'She found me afterwards and thanked me for helping to handle the emergency. She seems lovely. She's very beautiful and talented—I've read a few of her books.'

Joe nodded. 'She is all of those things.' *As are you.*

His mind veered close to disintegration as his worlds, past and present, desires and despair collided. He had to stay strong, as he'd always been. He couldn't fall apart then and he couldn't succumb to emotion now.

'Thanks for the offer, but there's nothing to talk about.' He changed lanes and put his foot down as the familiar shame made his hair stand on end. 'I was an absent father. My daughter died. My marriage couldn't survive. End of story.' His tight throat strangled his voice. He'd passed the point of wanting to impress Darcy. In fact, a part of him wanted to let go. To pour out his every ugly, loathsome feeling and see what she'd do with the mess.

'You were *not* an absent father.' The force of her vehemence startled him.

'How would you know?'

'I know because I had an absent father, literally,' she continued, pain in her eyes. 'I still do.'

So this was the issue at the core of all her vulnerabilities. Was the man she described, the one clearly responsible for her self-doubts, the reason she pushed herself so hard? Did she need to feel worthy of his love? Was that why she'd given up on her fiancé too? To protect herself from being so…vulnerable?

He fought the rampant urge to ask her for all the details. What right did he have picking over her pain when he fiercely guarded his own?

'I'm sorry that you had that experience,' he said, hating the idea of Darcy being hurt.

'It's okay.' She stared at her lap, where her hands twisted. 'I'm better off without him, although it took me a lot of years to realise that.' She looked out of the window as they covered some miles back to the city, the traffic building and the fields of gold fading.

Joe ruminated over his own regrets, comparing himself, his desire to provide well for his family after growing up in relative hardship, to the painful picture of absent fatherhood Darcy painted.

'Was he ever in the picture?' he asked.

'My parents split before my first birthday. He visited sporadically for the first few years, took me places, brought gifts. Then as I grew older the visits dwindled to once a year. He always had a believable excuse, just enough of an explanation for me to feel somehow guilty for missing him. I had romantic childhood dreams that one day he'd come back for good, settle close and be a real father, like Grant, my stepfather,' she said, her wistful tone tugging at a place in Joe's chest that had become way too invested in her well-being. 'I spent hours lying on my bed, staring at my ceiling, waiting.'

She turned back to Joe, her eyes hard. 'Then I grew up.'

She sounded matter-of-fact, but he could see that the rejected little girl still resided inside Darcy. Joe ached to hold her. No one should experience that level of deep-rooted abandonment, constantly raised and then dashed hopes. Darcy was a bright and bubbly woman—warm, caring, funny. It was a privilege to know her. Who wouldn't want to be a part of her life?

Of course, she'd hate his sympathy as much as he'd refused hers.

'I know we haven't known each other that long, but you were a great father, Joe. Trust me. I saw the photos of you and your family when I used the bathroom earlier. You and Rosie adored each other—it's there in your eyes, in your smiles, in all those experiences you shared. You showed up, you cared and she knew you loved her; that's what matters.'

Joe's throat tightened until he considered pulling over in case he grew dizzy. Yes, he'd been there, largely, for the big days. The birthdays and Christmases, the first day of every school year and the annual holidays. But he hadn't been there for all of the little things, the everyday moments. He'd been too focused on his career aspirations, in part to provide for Laura and Rosie and give them the best life he could, but also to fulfil the needs of his ego. Now he ached with how much he wished he could turn back the clock and relive every ordinary second better, cherish the little things, the quiet moments, the beautifully mundane.

'I spent too much time at work for stupid superficial reasons,' he admitted, his throat raw.

Darcy shook her head, as if confident in her

belief. 'Wanting a career and excelling at it isn't stupid.'

'Maybe, but my main motivation was to take financial care of my family. After my father died my mother struggled to be the breadwinner and the single parent to my sister and me. I vowed to do better, to provide well, to ensure my family had more. And for what? It was all pointless. I lost all that was important.'

'You did your family proud—your home was beautiful and, by the looks of those photos, you gave Rosie a wonderful childhood full of laughter and rich experiences.'

Joe's heart stuttered painfully as he thought of the photos Darcy referred to. Rosie had been the happy, vibrant girl Darcy saw. She'd loved to tease Joe and always had some scheme on the go, be it to enlist his help with her latest craft project or game of hide and seek, the rooms of that family home he'd once occupied alive with chatter and giggles.

He glanced Darcy's way, marvelling at her sharp observation and intuition, wondering what kind of little girl she'd been. Just having her at his former home had made him want things—things he'd long ago sworn off. Even before the emergency he'd wanted to leave, to take Darcy with him and escape the place where he felt the biggest failure of all. His past. She grounded him somehow. Made him feel more like his old self. Oh, he'd never be whole again, but Darcy's presence, the way she looked at him, the way she asked his opinion and advice without taking any of his nonsense…it made him glimpse a part of the man he'd been for a while, as if discovering a dusty old photograph.

At his silence, Darcy continued. 'All parents worry about balance. That doesn't make you a bad person. It doesn't mean you were negligent or in any way to blame. Rosie had leukaemia.'

'I went overboard.' He clenched his teeth, spurred on now that he'd started to expose his ugly parts. 'I became lured by the long hours and the personal gratification of my job. Pushing myself for the next promotion, consumed by the responsibility and the knowledge that I was needed, making a difference.' Joe cast her a cautious look. 'I think you might understand how that feels.'

Darcy gave a small hesitant nod. 'There's nothing wrong with being good at your job.'

'No, there isn't, as long as it's for the right reasons. But let my life be a cautionary tale of ambition and what truly matters. Yes, I once had it all, but I'm also living proof of how quickly it can all vanish.'

Darcy touched his arm and his body shuddered at the glimmer of pleasure.

'It wasn't your fault, Joe.'

He looked away from her compassion-darkened stare.

She was right. Sadly, knowing that didn't help in the slightest.

CHAPTER EIGHT

DANGER SLITHERED OVER Darcy's skin like the lick of a flame as Joe parked outside her flat in the vacant space that her sister usually used. She should get out of his car, thank him for the lift and watch him drive away, because her wants and needs were overwhelming.

The house was dark, empty. Stella was working a late shift at the hospital.

'Do you want to come in?' she asked, irresistibly drawn to this open version of Joe.

His heartbreaking confession during the ride back to London had ignited not only her innate compassion but also deepened the connection she felt. She'd had to sit on her hands for the rest of the journey in order to stop herself from taking him in her arms and holding him tight. Now, she wasn't ready to say goodbye, even though she should—she wanted him close after such an intensely fraught day.

Just for a little longer.

Darcy risked a sideways glance, immediately regretting it. His hair was ruffled where he'd run his fingers through it. A dark shadow of sexy stubble covered his jaw. And his eyes… So many emotions swam in their dark brown depths, Darcy felt at risk of drowning. He looked so conflicted, as if he were two men, two sides of a coin. A man who looked at her with desire, the same man she admired and respected at the hospital, and the shadow of that man. Hurting, tortured, punishing himself.

How could she resist that call? Her woman's heart wanted him with similar desire and the doctor in her yearned to help him heal. Darcy was a giver, empathetic. She was fulfilled by reaching out, human to human.

But that was all it could be for them. Physical—yes. Practical—all good. Emotional—no way.

Joe hesitated. *Sensible man.*

Darcy saw potential risk stamped all over him, but surely if she kept her head, indulged only in her attraction and ignored the way he made her crave more, she'd be safe, especially away from work. She'd given her career her all since her split from Dean and she was almost there, at the top of the mountain. She and Joe had an expiry date. Soon she'd move on and likely never see him again.

He'd made a valid point about priorities and

the importance of family and work/life balance. Darcy drove herself hard, set high standards and was goal oriented, but Joe had been wrong about one thing: she no longer wanted it all. She'd put herself out there emotionally with Dean and it hadn't worked out, although with the tumult of her feelings for Joe racing around her head she belatedly realised that she perhaps hadn't committed her all to her previous relationship.

There was a part of her that had entered into it with pretty low expectations, as if waiting for it to fail. And, like all good self-fulfilling prophesies, it had.

But a relationship was the last thing on her mind.

She craved the return of the visceral bond they'd shared when Joe had reached for her hand, the pride that lit her up like a firework when he'd looked to her for reassurance while they'd worked side by side to save Holly. He'd shown her that he valued her medical skills.

'It's been a moving day, and I make a mean cup of tea if that will sway you.' She tried to keep things light. Perhaps he'd open up even more. Perhaps she could help him unravel his regrets. She wanted to understand why he punished himself for what was surely a great and unfair tragedy but definitely not his fault, because she sensed that he didn't believe in his own innocence.

Joe smiled, his gaze both lost and somehow searching in a way that lured Darcy, physically and emotionally, the way lungs needed oxygen. 'Tea would be great, thanks.'

He killed the engine and unclipped his seat belt, his T-shirt rising up to expose a strip of toned abdomen, the sight of which left Darcy salivating. At her front door she fumbled with her key in the lock, her heart pitter-pattering in anticipation and fear of them being alone in her empty flat.

Darcy breathed through the panic of her ill-judged invitation. Already she had a head full of erotic visions involving Joe, except now that they'd worked as a team to save Holly, now that he'd needed her in a moment of alarm… that meant something more to her than the physical attraction there since that first day they'd met.

Did he see her as an equal?

In the kitchen Darcy dropped her bag, flicked on the lights and then the kettle. She reached overhead for two mugs with jittery fingers, the hair at the nape of her neck rising with awareness of Joe in her kitchen, filling her personal space with his magnetic aura. When she turned to face him, prepared to fake a bright smile and make small talk or resurrect the personal conversation they'd begun in the car, he'd stepped closer.

Face to face, a mere pace apart.

Darcy fell into the depths of Joe's stare and all thoughts of conversation dispersed.

Heartbeats pulsed through her like lightning strikes, marking the seconds they stood in tense silence.

He raised his arm, slow and steady, to brush back that stubborn lock of her hair determined to reside on her cheek.

As if conditioned to his touch, Darcy turned her face into his palm, part of her craving more, craving it all. 'Joe...' His name passed her lips, all breathy and pleading. For what? She wanted him physically, of course, but they had complication written all over them, the space between them an emotional and professional minefield.

He was still grieving the death of his daughter and perhaps even the demise of his marriage, and before meeting him she'd sworn to focus on her career, a career she stood to jeopardise if they started something personal. Even sex would be a far from straightforward exchange between two people who shared insatiable chemistry, for good or bad. Come Monday morning she'd have to face him; he'd still be her boss. She needed his reference for her consultant position applications.

Could she risk clouding their work dynamic just for sex?

'I want you,' he said, his expression starkly open and honest.

Overwhelming need built inside Darcy, its pressure centred between her legs.

'I've tried to resist,' he said, his voice full of gravel, 'but I'm failing badly.'

Darcy wavered. Joe's eyes brimmed with repressed emotion. He was clearly experiencing the same conflict tugging Darcy in two different directions.

If only they were strangers. If only they'd met in a nightclub and shared a passionate one-night stand…

Darcy's eyes fluttered closed, defending herself against his intense stare and the call it issued. 'Me, too.' The release of admitting her feelings rushed her bloodstream like a potent shot of morphine. 'But…this isn't a good idea.'

She clamped her hand over her mouth—she'd spoken that aloud. It waved the red flag and her body, the neediness for his kiss, his touch, hated her for the unguarded outburst. Her eyelids blinked open to find Joe resolute, his jaw set, his eyes ablaze with desire.

As if deciding to swim against the tide and face the consequences when they reached the shore, they lunged for each other in unison. Their kiss landed, lips colliding, a desperate union of people who'd fought their hunger for too long.

The catharsis after all of the denial and reasoning, confusion and conflicted feelings almost buckled Darcy's knees. Joe's strong arms scooped around her waist, as if he sensed the physical cost of her surrender. Darcy's hands clawed at his wide shoulders, dragging him those last few millimetres closer.

'Darcy,' he grunted against her sensitive lips as he tightened his grip and hauled her body up his firm chest until she was balanced on tiptoes. Darcy parted her lips to the invasion of his tongue, the sensual glide making all the difference to her inflamed libido, which sparked and fizzed like a lit fuse.

Unlike the kiss in the on-call staffroom, which had been angry and full of frustration, this kiss exploded with pure, uncontrolled passion, blast after blast in a chain reaction that left Darcy a slave only to her body's needs. She weakened against Joe's strength and hardness. Through the lust fog in her head, she grew aware of movement and felt the edge of the kitchen table against the back of her thighs.

Fantastic idea.

She jumped up and spread her legs so that Joe's hips could slot into place. They fitted so perfectly she wanted to weep. How could something that felt this right be a bad idea? It was just sex, chemistry, a release. This tension had been brewing between them from day one.

A sense of blissful inevitable release washed over Darcy. Her fingers curled in his silky hair, his stubble rough against her palm as she kept him where her lips wanted him.

The shock of his warm palm on her thigh, where her dress had ridden up, added fire to her veins. She shunted her hips to the edge of the table, needing more friction, needing him closer, needing to feel him on every part of her body at once. His other hand skimmed her waist and travelled up her ribs to her breast and she tore her mouth away from his and opened her eyes, lost in his pleasure-darkened stare.

This was happening. They were doing this, crossing the line that kept them safely out of reach. Joe's handsome face was cloaked in arousal that made Darcy applaud her instincts. Their panting breaths mingled, their lips only a whisper apart.

'I wanted you from the start.' Joe cupped her breast, his thumb tracing the sensitive peak through her dress.

Darcy gasped at the sublime and foreign contact. It was as if she'd never been with a man before. His touch combined with his bold stare and stark declaration felt so good she knew this must be the worst idea she'd ever had. As Joe's erection pressed between her legs, she dredged her conscience, searching for the inner strength to pause and reflect.

Yes, it was just sex, and they were adults, capable of keeping things professional at work, no matter what happened here between them tonight.

But…

This day carried momentous significance for Joe. It wouldn't be just sex, not today, and Darcy couldn't afford for it to be anything more.

She pressed her mouth back to his in denial, trying to shut out the anguish she'd seen in his eyes when he'd talked about his daughter, when he'd looked at Darcy with both relief and despair after successfully resuscitating Holly. He'd been so haunted it hurt Darcy's soul.

Hating herself, she pulled back and searched his heated gaze for what she knew she'd find there—the one thing that would stop this where her willpower and common sense had failed miserably.

Grief shone through the desire. A warning light, glaring, blinding.

She couldn't do it. Selfishness was not a part of her nature. She cared about Joe too much to take advantage of his vulnerable state, and she couldn't have him resent her down the track.

She needed him. At work, for his expertise and training and as a person she admired, liked, respected.

She placed her hands on his chest and gently pushed. 'Stop. We need to stop.'

Her body rebelled, flames leaping over her skin. She slid from the edge of the table, her breasts grazing his chest and his delicious scent a cloud of temptation from which there was no escape.

To Darcy's shame, there was also an aftertaste of relief as she withdrew from the emotional temptation of Joe's pain. Taking care of herself didn't come naturally, but she'd vowed, after Dean, that her career must take priority. It was her chance to lay all of her own demons to rest. To finally make it and know that she was good enough, despite the trials that had shaped her.

Face taut with confusion and resignation, Joe backed up. His warm touch left her so rapidly she shivered.

He speared his fingers through his chaotic hair. 'Hell...yes. You're right.'

No...convince me I'm wrong...convince me that it's just sex.

'I don't want to be right,' she choked out, guilt that she'd not only allowed things to go so far, but she'd also rejected him when she knew the size and shape of that emotion so well gripping her vocal cords. 'I don't want this to be a bad idea, but sense tells me it is.'

Grief was such a complex process. She couldn't bear to bring up the subject of Rosie when his mouth was still bruised from their kisses, his arousal still pushing at the fly of his jeans.

'What about Monday, at work?' she said, trying to reason her way back to some semblance of normal when she felt anything but. No matter how much her libido hated her right now, this was the right decision.

Joe's grief and pain must be amplified after today's party.

Darcy pushed down her dress, self-conscious and suddenly cold. 'It feels like I'd be…taking advantage.' She hesitated. Joe would hate to think she was motivated by pity. 'Today was rough, for many reasons… I just—'

'No, you're right,' he interrupted. 'It was rough.' He tugged at his hair. 'I am all over the place.' He set about composing himself, tugging the hem of his T-shirt and scrubbing a hand over his face.

Darcy looked away to give him some privacy. Her heart broke for him. He clearly blamed and punished himself for his daughter's death, but he deserved the happiness and healing his ex had found. She ached for herself too—she struggled with trust, and one of the reasons she was so drawn to Joe, beyond the fact that he was so sexy, was his integrity. She had to stop herself from grabbing him again, kissing him again and forcing the insight and compassion from her mind, acting purely on sensation, taking everything she wanted right here, right now on her kitchen table. To hell with the consequences.

But she couldn't risk the emotional outpouring she suspected would follow. She couldn't sleep with him *and* care. It was too risky.

'I should go.' He headed for the door.

'Wait.' She had no idea what she wanted to say; she just needed him to understand. 'Joe, I want to be there for you.'

Joe winced as if she'd insulted him. 'Just not for casual sex… I get it.'

'No… Yes…' Horrified, she sought the right words. 'Casual sex is all we can have. I've tried to have more than that in the past, and right now… I need to focus on myself, my career. I just don't think we should make such a momentous decision to cross the line when you might be lonely or reeling from a tough day.'

Who was she trying to kid? There was no one lonelier than her.

Apart from her sisters, with whom she'd once, as a little girl, felt like the odd one out, she had few friends. She'd always told herself she was too busy with work. But, in truth, she either held herself distant or pushed people away before she could be hurt, the way her father had hurt her. Again and again. She'd even withdrawn from Dean the minute he'd proposed. At the time she'd convinced herself it just didn't feel right, that their differences were insurmountable, but now she suspected she'd been predominantly motivated by the fear of possible future rejection.

Joe's expression had turned granite-hard.

Darcy flushed. 'Sorry… I didn't mean the lonely comment… I just… I think this needs more thought than either of us has given it. Don't you agree?' This must be a big deal for him if he hadn't dated since his divorce. It was a big deal for *her*. She could allow herself a casual fling, but she couldn't become distracted at the final career hurdle. She'd worked too hard. And the way she'd become ensnared by caring for Joe and wanting to help him, the risks of emotional entanglement were amplified.

Joe held her eye contact so she felt naked, exposed. 'I've thought about it plenty,' he said with soul-searing honesty. 'But you're right about the timing; this was…ill-judged.'

He pressed his gorgeous lips together, and Darcy's stomach plummeted. She wanted them back on hers, wanted to rewind and keep her mouth shut, keep every one of his kisses and lose herself in pleasure.

'I'm sorry, Joe.' Her throat ached. 'I want you, but I don't want to hurt you.' Or herself. 'You're punishing yourself enough as it is.'

His grim smile cut like a knife. 'I understand. This is why I didn't initially tell you about Rosie, why I shouldn't have opened up to you in the car, because now I'm no longer a man you're attracted to; I'm just a man who can't get over the fact that his daughter died.'

He hardened his jaw, and Darcy almost caved and begged him to forget the last few minutes.

'I wanted to be that first guy for a while, that's all...' He shrugged.

And then he left, taking with him a tiny piece of Darcy's heart.

CHAPTER NINE

A WEEK LATER Joe forced his eyes to linger on the city lights of Amsterdam beyond the window of the swanky Italian restaurant while the conversation around the table droned on. He curled his fingers into a loose fist where his hand rested on his thigh. Only a few inches separated his thigh from Darcy's. A few promise-filled inches that might as well be an entire universe.

His regret returned full force like a blow to the chest, winding him.

She'd been right to call a halt that night a week ago. Right to declare them complicated. Right to worry about any fallout from a reckless affair that might affect her career.

And he *was* punishing himself, or he had been before she'd pulled him up on that, forcing him to examine the contents of his head and acknowledge that he was stuck, suspended in his grief, because to acknowledge any positive feelings like those he'd experienced since Darcy had blasted into his life, to move on as Laura had done, shot panic through him like white-hot laser beams.

What if he allowed himself joy? Would that diminish or invalidate his love for Rosie somehow?

Wasn't a part of him relieved when Darcy had applied the brakes? Because a distraction that good, letting go of his pain and embracing his out-of-control attraction to Darcy, might change him, or make him forget.

Not that sex could heal, of course, but he'd started to care about Darcy. It wouldn't, couldn't, be just sex. Was he strong enough to keep those emotions off the table?

He'd certainly clung to his pain for so long—it was his only connection to Rosie.

Except all of this self-reflection hadn't lessened his desire for the woman he craved day and night, the woman sitting next to him now. Her delicate scent and the rich timbre of her voice dragged him from his thoughts. Spending time with her equated to a kind of torture.

Restlessness coiled in his stomach as he tuned back in to the largely medical chat happening around the table. He and Darcy were attending a conference—the European Surgical Innovation Summit. Ever since they'd left London he'd wanted Darcy to himself. He wanted to show her that he was more than a damaged man in need of her compassion. That she'd been the one responsible for waking that dormant side of his masculinity. That she was wrong; he could separate sex from his emotional life because, no matter how much he cared about Darcy, the woman he'd come to know and respect, sex was all that he could offer. The rest of him was all tied up.

'You're drifting off again,' she side whispered in his direction, a playful smile tugging at her gorgeous mouth, reminding him of frantic kisses and the way his arousal had sought the heat between her thighs.

Joe grinned, casting her a wink for good measure; he actually winked. All day they'd achieved a lighter, flirty vibe. Being away from the hospital changed their dynamic enough that they could be more open and honest, more real without professional restriction.

It was a revelation. Joe hadn't felt so…joyful for years.

'I've heard all these chats before,' he whispered, inhaling her warm Darcy aroma. And he'd had to share the one person he wanted to talk to—her.

He checked his watch, desperate to get her alone. They'd never had that coffee date.

'Was that your excuse for inattention during the lectures today?' she said, calling Joe out with a knowing look. Away from work she was relaxed and flirtatious. It gave him hope that they could work this out in a mutually beneficial way.

He shrugged. ‘You noticed that, huh?’ He’d barely heard a word of the varied and informative presentations today, ones he’d anticipated with interest before meeting Darcy, because she’d been at his side. All day. A constant distraction, a reminder of that seriously heated session in her kitchen and all of the almost moments in between then and now.

He hadn’t felt that wild loss of inhibition for decades, since he was a teenager. For a moment when she’d pulled back he’d been utterly dazed, so lost was he in the blissful oblivion of the physical pressure valve release.

He looked away from the temptation of her teasing stare. Darcy deserved more than his uncontrolled lust, more than he had to give.

But she didn’t want more. She wanted just sex. That she wanted him at all in all his ugly, broken glory was miracle enough. And once the emotional turmoil in him had settled the next day he’d almost driven back to her place, hammered down the door and presented himself as the ideal casual sex candidate.

Only the honest part of him knew his feelings were already engaged. He cared that she’d been hurt by her father in the past. Now he simply hoped he could hide those feelings and take what was on offer.

Joe watched her lips caress the tines of the fork as she ate. The urge to touch her, kiss her, explore every inch of her body overwhelmed him once more, an itch along his spine that he couldn't quite reach.

'How did you find the symposium?' he asked, dragging himself back to a professional footing.

'Are you asking as my boss?' she said. 'Because then my answer would be: it was extremely useful and professionally enlightening.' She raised her eyebrows in that taunting way of hers that never failed to make Joe's heart race.

He lowered his voice. 'What if I'm asking as the guy you made tea for on Saturday evening?' He shouldn't raise this subject, especially not here, in front of colleagues, but the flecks of silver in her irises which sparkled in the candlelight spurred him on. He was done pretending. To her, to himself. Time to lay his cards on the table.

'Ah…' She smiled, a hint of colour in her cheeks. 'Well, to him, I'd have to confess I was somewhat…distracted, too. By the guy sitting next to me.'

Joe latched onto her stare, his blood rushing around his body. 'Perhaps you're tired,' he said, playing along. 'We've had a busy week at City.'

'Maybe a little. My boss is this extreme perfectionist, demanding an even greater standard than I put on myself, which is up there.' She raised her hand overhead, indicating what he already knew. Now he wanted her to know that, no matter what had happened in her past, she needn't try so hard, that she was enough exactly as she was—perfect.

'Guy sounds like a jerk with nothing else in his life but work.' Joe smiled when he really wanted to take her hand. 'Don't be like that guy.'

'Oh, he can be…challenging.' Her mouth twitched with mirth and Joe sucked on his bottom lip, remembering how her kisses tasted and the breathless quality of her soft moans. 'But he's a very dedicated and instinctive surgeon…' her eyes softened and his throat went dry '…so I can't help but respect him.'

Her words buzzed through his head. Joe sat frozen, mesmerised by what he saw in her stare, the understanding, the heat, the promise. The rest of the restaurant's patrons, including the handful of colleagues at their table, faded away, leaving just him and Darcy and…possibility.

Just then a surgeon Joe had known for years, Professor Jensen, who sat to Darcy's right, engaged her in conversation.

Joe pushed some pasta around his plate, trying not to eavesdrop but failing.

'Yes, I've read your paper on hepatic complications of bariatric surgery,' Jensen said. Joe's possessive side flickered to life. Of course, Jensen had made a beeline for the seat next to Darcy the minute the small group had entered the restaurant. The guy had a wife Darcy's age and a dreadful reputation for philandering. Joe's blood still simmered after he'd already monopolised her time over dinner.

'I found your review interesting,' Jensen continued, his pompous voice grating on Joe's nerves, 'if a little…sketchy in places,' he finished with a superior air, shovelling a forkful of pasta into his mouth.

Joe had attended many of these symposia over the years and had never found the man worthy of particular note in the past. Now he had the ludicrous urge to defend Darcy. The conference was over for the day. This was supposed to be a social event.

Joe sensed her stiffen slightly beside him. 'Yes, the nature of review articles, I fear, Professor Jensen, but thank you for your invaluable feedback.'

Joe concealed his ready grin against the rim of his water glass. Of course, Darcy knew how to put the old buffoon in his place without breaking a sweat. The man wouldn't win Darcy's sycophancy or flirtation. One of the things he admired most about her was her ability to straight talk, even with people who deemed themselves superior from time served in the profession.

He should keep his nose out of it but some irritation, perhaps that itch up his spine, the urge to get her alone, forced him to intercede.

'I found Ms Wright's review excellent, actually.' Joe caught the tiny shocked intake of Darcy's breath. 'She's certainly a great asset to my team. In fact, I hope to persuade her to co-author a paper I'm planning for *The Lancet* before she leaves for her consultant post.' He cast a glance sideways in time to see Jensen lose interest and address another colleague across the table.

He looked at Darcy. She hid her surprised expression behind one of mild censure. 'Thanks for sticking up for me,' she said in a hushed tone, 'but I had it in hand.'

'I know you did, but I couldn't stay silent.' She didn't need him to defend her against an egotistical professor looking to rattle a young, beautiful colleague so he could flex his intellectual muscle.

Except Joe couldn't help himself.

Her pressed together lips twitched, her mock sternness dissolving into a playful look full of delicious secrecy. 'Shh. He'll hear you.' Then she smiled her lovely relaxed smile and Joe breathed freely for the first time since they'd boarded the plane to Amsterdam.

They'd come a long way since their first tense

and prickly meeting when he'd been the one to ruffle her feathers. She trusted and respected him professionally and he valued her more than he could articulate.

Perhaps too much.

'Did you mean that?' she asked, glancing his way with hopeful curiosity. 'About the paper?' Darcy pushed away her half-full plate, her appetite clearly as non-existent as Joe's.

When could they politely get out of here?

'Of course. I've been meaning to raise the subject when I had a chance. Perhaps we can discuss it on the plane back to London tomorrow.'

She nodded, her eyes big expressive pools reflecting a whole raft of emotions he wanted to dissect. Did she still see him as an irritating boss? Or just a grieving father? Alone with Darcy, he felt as if he could be so much more. For the first time in years what he wanted had become crystal-clear.

Her.

'You didn't have to walk me back to the hotel,' she said, shivering slightly at Joe's proximity and pulling her cardigan closed over her chest.

'I wasn't going to let you walk the streets of Amsterdam alone,' he said, stepping closer so their arms almost touched. 'And I want to talk to you as much as I want to ensure that you're safe, for my own peace of mind. Would you like my jacket?'

She shook her head. Darcy's body trembles were down to full-blown anticipation. Especially when he looked at her the way he'd been doing all day, as if she were a dessert he wanted to devour.

Heaven help her…

'I've wanted to get you alone,' he said, placing his hand in the small of her back as the crowd of passers-by clogged the pavement. Not that she minded. Ever since she'd watched him drive away from her street she'd craved a return to this closeness. No matter how many times she'd reasoned that it was better if they never happened, she couldn't be convinced.

Darcy forced herself to breathe in something approximating a normal rhythm at his sure and resolute touch. 'Have you?'

Me, too, a voice yelled inside her head as she recalled the torture of being at his side most of the day but also surrounded by people. Because spending the day with Joe, away from their professional roles and with no emotional triggers to cloud the issue, she'd been consumed with him so she hardly knew the contents of her own sensible mind.

He glanced her way, his eye contact bold and steady, as if he knew exactly how paper-thin were her defences and arguments. 'Yes, I want to thank you for sensing my extreme vulnerability and kicking me out that night.'

Darcy's heart clenched at his honesty. The longer she knew Joe, the more she learned that what you saw was who he was. No games, no tactics, no hidden agenda. He'd sat next to her in the lecture theatre rather than sitting with consultant colleagues. He'd asked for her opinions on the topics presented and introduced her to the internationally renowned surgeons that he knew.

He'd even stood up for her to the self-important Professor Jensen. She couldn't recall the last time anyone had done that. Self-reliant Darcy could take care of herself, but it was nice to know that he cared.

'You're welcome.' She smiled and her cheeks ached; she'd smiled so much today. 'Although, at the time I regretted it immediately.'

Her breath stuttered in her chest at admitting how much she still wanted him. But she refused to enter this fling based on just common or garden lust. She cared about him as a person too much.

And you've never felt lust this powerful before.

Because things had changed. Finally, she felt like his professional equal, as if Joe understood her, respected her, valued her. Her whole life she'd craved the acceptance that she was okay, that she wasn't defective because of her father's repeated and confusing abandonment. To feel it from Joe, a man she respected in return, both personally for what he'd been through and professionally, brought a rush so powerful her head spun with yearning.

There was no longer any point denying her feelings for Joe. They must be written on her face. But if they were to cross the line that they'd only narrowly avoided last time, they'd need to do it together.

They paused at a zebra crossing and Joe placed his hand on her elbow as he scanned the traffic. She hid her smile. Joe was old-school, a gentleman, and she surprised herself with how much she liked the small signs that he cared for her well-being. It called to the part of her that craved his touch as if it were the oxygen she needed to breathe.

She could become seriously addicted to him.

A niggle of lingering doubt forced its way into her conscious thoughts. 'How have you been this week? I haven't liked to ask at the hospital, but I've been thinking about you.'

Darcy held her breath, wary of prying into his grief. Except his emotions, his feelings of loss, were normal and nothing to be ashamed of. It was human, understandable, expected. Could a parent ever get over the death of a child? She suspected not.

'I've been good. Thanks for asking.' He glanced her way, looking at her as if he wanted to say a whole lot more. As if he wanted to kiss her here under the Amsterdam streetlights.

Then he dragged in a breath, as if making a decision. 'You'll think I'm mad, but I've taken to talking to Rosie sometimes.'

Darcy's heart clenched, desperate to hold him. Instead, she reached for his hand and squeezed his fingers. 'I think that's lovely and completely normal.' Emotion clogged her throat but she swallowed it down, moved to show him that she understood.

'When I was a little girl I used to talk to my real father in my head at night. I'd pretend that he'd ask about my day at school, just like my stepfather did, or praise me for my artwork or spelling test results.'

Joe raised her hand to his mouth and pressed a kiss on the back of her hand. 'I'm sorry that he wasn't there for you. He doesn't deserve a daughter as wonderful as you.'

'You're right there.' The heat of tears threatened behind her eyes, not only for her own loss but for Joe's, too, because if ever there was a deserving father it was him. 'Sadly, I only discovered that years later, after repeated rejections. It took being let down again and again for the fantasy bubble I'd invented to burst.' Darcy shrugged, forgiving herself anew for her naive hopes.

This time Joe pulled her against him and pressed his lips to her forehead. 'You are perfect, a daughter anyone would be proud of. I bet your parents are.'

She laughed, snuggling into his chest and inhaling the clean and erotic scent of him and his shirt. 'My sisters and I are very high achievers.'

'Healthy sibling rivalry?' he asked.

She sobered as he struck an exposed nerve. 'Something like that, although for a while I convinced myself that I was the odd one out, because they had the same father where he'd only adopted me. It's silly, I know, and totally down to my messed-up way of thinking and nothing my family did.'

'That doesn't mean he loved you less,' said Joe with understanding in his eyes.

'No. He's a great dad; I'm lucky to have him. Sometimes I feel guilty, even bitter, that I might have held back from loving Grant completely out of a misguided sense of loyalty to my father.' That same part of her that held back had also felt not quite good enough, despite her wonderful upbringing.

They'd veered close to an emotional hotspot for both of them, Darcy suspected. For a short distance they walked hand in hand in pensive silence.

'About last weekend…' he said as the hotel came into view. 'I wouldn't want you to ever feel…used or convenient. That was never remotely my intention. I *was* in an emotional place that day, but I need you to know that I'm also a man—a man who wants you more than I have any right to.'

Darcy's pulse raced, speech almost deserting her. 'Joe… I see you that way, and I want you, too… I just needed us to make a clear-headed decision.' She didn't want to think about her complex situation with Dean when her head was filled with Joe, but she needed the reminder of their turbulent times, their fights and resentments, the way Darcy had often felt misunderstood or unappreciated, in order to guard her emotions and keep this explosive connection brewing between her and Joe light and temporary.

Except tonight she wondered if it was a warning she needed more than Joe.

'I understand—it's just sex.' Heat flared in his stare and deepened the tone of his voice. 'Neither of us is looking for more.'

She nodded, her stomach strangely hollow when she should feel nothing but relief and excitement. 'I need to focus on my upcoming consultant job interviews and I'll be moving on in a couple of months...'

Joe nodded. 'We're both mature and dedicated enough to safeguard our work above all else. We're on the same page.'

Joe was saying all the right things. She wanted to sleep with him. Yes, it was risky, it could potentially alter their professional relationship, but her libido didn't care one jot. Even her intellect was struggling to mount coherent objections now they'd established the rules and found themselves back where they'd always been: undeniably attracted to each other.

As for her other feelings for Joe, it was natural to care about someone she liked and admired so much, but surely she could set that aside for one stolen night...

They crossed the threshold of the hotel and Darcy dropped his hand to press the button for the lift. It was now or never, sink or swim. She risked a look in his direction and all but spontaneously combusted from the look of sheer need in Joe's eyes.

'So you're saying you'd accept if I invited you to my room?' She tried to exhibit the same cool pragmatism while her insides had turned molten. But she needed to approach this fling with the same calm rationale she gave to her career moves and clinical decisions. She'd chosen that career over a relationship in the past.

Unlike her ex, this man understood the sacrifices required to succeed at this job. He wouldn't make her choose, and he couldn't let her down because she had no expectations beyond tonight.

He stepped closer, his own feelings on the matter clear in the intensity of his stare and the increase in his breathing rate. 'Look at me,' he said. 'You'll see my answer.'

He swallowed, and Darcy saw the cost of his vulnerability, his ceding control. He wanted her and she'd exhausted all of her excuses.

Tonight, he wasn't her boss. He wasn't a man wrapped up in grief. He was Joe.

In silent agreement they stepped inside the lift.

To her dismay, they weren't alone for the journey to the fourth floor. Had they been, Darcy might have succumbed to the urgent need to leap at Joe and kiss him the way he'd kissed her last Saturday. From the look of polite impatience on his face, Joe might have pressed her up against the wall the way he'd pressed her back into her kitchen table, his hard body commanding, his control barely leashed, his need for her decimating all else.

The furnace built inside Darcy until she was certain her face glowed. Their lift companion smiled as Darcy and Joe exited on Darcy's floor, telling her that sexual tension cloaked them like a fog. Every step Darcy took trembled with urgency.

Inside her hotel room, Darcy dropped Joe's hand and placed her bag on the desk. She needed a moment to slow the crazy swirls of desire making her dizzy.

She sensed his body heat at her back and her knees weakened. She spun slowly to face him, needing to spell out her terms and conditions. For her sanity or for his benefit?

'Just tonight,' she said, although it came out as a whisper. 'We can't let this affect working together.'

He hadn't touched her again since letting go of her hand in the lift, but her skin was aflame, her blood supercharged as it raced around her trembling body.

'I agree.' His stare devoured her. 'But if you've changed your mind…'

'No.' She'd die if he left her now. 'I haven't changed my mind.' She stepped closer, reached for his hand and squeezed, to comfort herself more than him, to stop his escape, although his eyes told her everything she needed to know about Joe's wants and intentions.

'I want this,' she whispered in confirmation. He understood her. He accepted her just the way she was, and she recognised the limits to what he could offer. They weren't embarking on a relationship. It was just one night. They'd quench this insane attraction and move on as if tonight had never happened.

Darcy forced herself to ignore the trickle of cold in her veins at that idea. Before she could reach for him, Joe cupped her face, his thumbs tracing her cheekbones with aching slowness. Darcy stared into his eyes until her vision swam and her heart pounded almost out of her chest. Perhaps *Wham-bam, thank you, ma'am* would have been better than this slow, seductive burn they generated. She wanted to tear his clothes off, but she also wanted to honour that they'd have only one night. That they'd needed time to process their feelings after their last encounter when she'd slammed on the brakes. That she needed time to slow the frantic race of her pulse and ensure she kept her emotions off the table, focus only on the way he made her feel physically.

Already she felt close to disintegration and they'd barely touched.

She circled her hands around his wrists, clinging to him for balance. 'Kiss me, Joe. Kiss me the way you wanted to the other night. I won't stop you this time.'

As if waiting for her permission, he unleashed himself with the same steady and meticulous attention to detail that he applied at the hospital.

His fingers speared her hair and dug into the back of her scalp. His strong thigh stepped between her legs and his lips settled over hers, slow and sensual, consuming her every sense, commanding her body in a kiss that felt way more than a kiss.

A melding of two imperfect people who understood the limitations of the other. It was so freeing that Darcy practically levitated.

Joe slanted his mouth over hers and she yielded on a gasp, lips parting to the welcome invasion of his tongue. He backed her up against the desk, scooping one arm around her waist to hoist her from the floor and deposit her on the surface. They momentarily broke apart while Darcy spread her legs and impatiently tugged the belt loops on his jeans to bring him closer.

'I can't stop wanting you,' he said, his voice cracking as he trailed kisses over her jaw and down her neck until her eyes rolled back at the delicious sensations, which were amplified by his heartfelt admission.

'Me neither… I've tried.' Oh, how she'd tried. Since day one she'd done her best to hate him, ignore him, dismiss him and resist him. Look where all that fight had ended.

Right here in his arms, sharing his kisses, wanting more, so much more.

He nodded. Clearly, they'd been trapped in

limbo together, each battling this, battling themselves, battling their pasts. But now that they'd laid down the rules and showed mutual trust and respect, surrender felt harmless.

It was perfect.

Passion without consequences.

No longer willing to wait another minute for her reward after the denial she'd suffered these past weeks, Darcy hurriedly unbuttoned Joe's casual shirt. The fabric smelled of detergent and of Joe, but when her palms skated over the smooth warm skin, the ridges and dips of his abdomen and the soft hair of his chest, she closed her eyes against the heady rush of overwhelming sensation.

With a bone-dry swallow, Darcy leaned back to look her fill, tracing every defined muscle with her unapologetic stare. He was beautiful, so sexy she wanted to photograph him for posterity. Her keen doctor's eye mapped the anatomical landmarks of his male perfection, and she spotted a scar across one of his ribs. She traced the slight bump with her fingertip, fascinated because it was Joe she was touching and everything about him was new and compelling.

If only his emotional wounds could heal so easily. If only he'd stop blaming himself, stop clinging to his pain… Perhaps then he'd be ready to allow himself the happiness he deserved.

He removed her hand and lifted it to his mouth, kissing her fingertips and then the inside of her wrist where her pulse fluttered.

'It's from a chest drain,' he explained. 'I broke a rib playing rugby at school—ended up with a pneumothorax.' He rolled his eyes and grinned, his lips still pressed to her sensitive skin so that electricity skittered along her nerves.

Darcy shuddered the way she had when he'd cupped her breast on Saturday, her whole body reacting to his smile, which occasionally, like now, reached his eyes with blinding effect.

How could he do this to her? Undo her so effortlessly with a single self-deprecating smile?

Because this proud, capable, life-saving man had made himself vulnerable to her, shared his deepest regrets and made her feel that she wasn't alone with her own demons.

She cupped his face, his stubble scraping her palm. She wanted to kiss him from head to toe. To taste his skin, find his ticklish spots, soothe away the lines from around his eyes, unless they accompanied that devastating smile.

Reminding herself that this was about sex only, Darcy slid from the table and lifted her dress over her head, tossing it away. She flicked her sandals from her feet and unclasped her bra, her body warming and her belly fluttering at Joe's appreciative stare.

His expression grew more serious with every passing second. His nostrils flared, his eyes raked her near nakedness, telling Darcy what it cost him to keep his hands to himself. Instead of touching her, he removed his jeans and shoes and socks, matching Darcy item for item until their clothing lay in a heap.

'You're so beautiful,' he whispered huskily and then stepped close once more. His feverish skin made contact with hers, inch by inch, flames licking at the points of contact.

'So are you,' she croaked, recalling the sight of his thick muscular thighs and the rigid length of him behind tight black boxers. 'I have a condom,' she said, reaching behind her for her bag, ever the practical, safety-conscious doctor.

'So do I.' Joe raised his eyebrows and smiled his dazzling smile. 'What a team we make.'

They laughed together and then he grew serious, tugged her close and took her mouth in another heated kiss that left Darcy weak-kneed.

What a team we make. If only he knew what those words meant to her.

CHAPTER TEN

JOE PRAYED DARCY couldn't feel the trembles racking his body as he laid her back against the cool white sheets of the hotel bed. Every muscle in his body screamed at him to speed this up, to surrender to his base desires, which had been tightly coiled like a rusty spring and ignored these past four years, and lose control of his powerful desire for this woman. But another part, the part of his brain still functioning, knew instinctively to cherish every second of tonight, as that was all they'd have. Tomorrow, they'd go back to London, pretend this had never happened, their chaste workplace dynamic restored. He her boss and she his junior.

Because, no matter how good she felt in his arms, no matter that he'd never felt more alive, more optimistic, more like himself, he had nothing more than this to give. Relationships took time and commitment and posed a massive potential risk for crushing heartache. All of Joe's energy was consumed by work and remembering, honouring and grieving Rosie.

A flicker of hesitation made it to the functioning part of his brain. He didn't want to hurt Darcy, or mislead her. But he'd been as upfront as he could, and she knew what she wanted—one night. He'd never met anyone more certain of her path.

'How did I get so lucky?' he asked, covering her sublime body with his, marvelling at the softness of her skin, the hunger in her passion-glazed stare and the sexy splay of her silky hair across the pillow. He wanted to bury his face in the golden strands and inhale her unique Darcy scent, commit it to memory, because he'd want to remember tonight, this amazing woman who somehow brought a flicker of life back to his battle-weary heart.

Instead, he kissed her once more, consoling himself by tangling his fingers through her hair while he trailed his lips down her neck.

'Joe,' she moaned, her breathtaking face soft with desire. Desire for him. This smart, funny, dedicated woman saw something worthwhile in him, despite his broken pieces.

She understood his crazier moments—he'd never told another soul how he still talked to his dead daughter as if she were still with him, not even Laura. She laughed at him when he took himself too seriously. And for all she'd been through growing up—feeling rejected by the one man who was supposed to love her unconditionally—she wasn't afraid to be vulnerable with him. Now he understood her constant need to prove herself and how it helped her to reach her career goals. But some part of him wondered if it wasn't holding her back from being happy, fulfilled.

Darcy's hips rocked under him, reminding him that Darcy's happiness wasn't his business, at least not beyond tonight. Her fingernails bit into his upper arms, dragging his mind back to the physical sensations he could indulge. A great wave of desire rose up inside him at the sight of her parted lips, her slumberous eyes, her passion. She needed him in this second, this strong, independent woman, but somehow she also held him together with her fearless forthright tenacity.

Joe bent to suck her nipple, loving the whimpers he drew from her throat and the way she gripped his hips with her thighs. Hunger roared through him, splintering him apart. How had he done without a connection like this for so long? Darcy had given him back this vital side of his maleness. He'd never forget that gift. The least he could do was rock her world and give her a night to remember when she moved on.

Done being patient, Joe knelt back on his

haunches and slid her underwear down her legs. 'We might need to take this slowly,' he said. 'I'm a bit rusty.'

He wasn't certain how long he'd last after four years of abstinence, but he'd been none too shabby at this in his heyday. He likely still had the moves.

She chuckled, cupping his face. 'Me, too—let's take all night.'

His heart surged with renewed vigour. Could she be any more perfect? He kissed her again, his hand sliding between her thighs to the slickness there. She gripped his wrist and held him in place, her hips rocking in rhythm, telling him she liked his moves just fine.

Joe's wicked side roared to life and he dipped his head, murmuring, 'We are so unprofessional. What would our patients think?' He took her nipple back into his mouth and watched desire flicker across her features, colour blooming under her skin.

'Yes…'

He wasn't sure if she was agreeing with his statement, encouraging him or both, but he kept up his attentions, a man on a mission. When she shattered, he kissed up her cries and rode out every second of her pleasure at her side, privilege soaring in his chest until he felt like a king.

Finally spent, Darcy threw her arms up over

her head, looked into his eyes and grinned. Then she laughed, a throaty, sexy laugh filled with delight. 'Oh…wow…' She giggled some more and Joe had to hide his own smile.

'That was funny?' Amusement spread, twitching at his lips, his spirit so light he struggled to recall if he'd ever felt so…euphoric.

'Amazing,' she said, tugging his mouth back to hers and peppering his face with kisses. 'You. Are. Amazing.' She stretched like a contented cat.

'Plenty more where that came from.' He winked, fresh urgency clawing at the layers of levity she wrapped around his heart. Of all the fantasies he'd had about this moment, he'd never once expected to laugh, to feel frivolity, but wonderful, beautiful Darcy brought that to the surface.

Darcy took him by surprise anew, shoving him flat on his back and straddling his hips. 'Don't make promises you can't keep,' she said, her voice sexy and husky. 'You said you were rusty before.'

Joe grinned, reached for the condom. 'Haven't you learned by now that I'm sometimes full of nonsense?'

Darcy laughed, nodded vigorously and then trailed distracting kisses over his chest.

Joe covered himself with the condom, his hands shaking with the effort of taking his time.

She was driving him crazy, that sensual mouth of hers finding all his erogenous zones. Done being passive, he cupped her hips, positioning her over him, where he wanted her.

'But I never break a promise.' He stared up at her to see mischief light her eyes.

'Don't worry,' she whispered, temptation itself, as she jutted out her breasts. 'You said it yourself—we're a team. Why should you do all the work?' She took him inside her with frustrating slowness that tested his limits to the max.

Heat boiled in his veins. She felt so good. 'Darcy…' he warned, fearful for his out-of-practice stamina. She bit down on her bottom lip and watched him with pleasure-drunk eyes. She was gorgeously dishevelled, flushed, her hair a wild tumble. He momentarily closed his eyes against the perfect vision, his chest crushed with too many feelings that he should have expected.

From day one this woman had challenged him, surprised him and somehow saw deep inside him. Of course, she'd be an almost overwhelming, hard to resist combination.

Biting the inside of his cheek to stave off the rush of pleasure as she began to rock her hips in a sensual glide, he closed his eyes once more. He wanted to see everything, feel everything, savour everything. But he also needed to keep a measure of mental distance from this incredible sexual experience. To remind himself that he couldn't get used to this degree of rapture. That a part of him, the part he couldn't forgive, didn't deserve such a life-enhancing experience as having Darcy in his arms, riding him, consuming every sense he possessed.

He'd always imagined himself a man of strength but, weak to Darcy's lure, he slammed his eyes back open in order to watch.

'Joe… You feel so good.' She braced her palms flat on his chest, her hair falling forward in two golden curtains framing her stunning face.

Joe forced his hands to stay curled into fists at her hips, fought the battle to take every scrap of pleasure she'd give him, to touch every inch of her and lose himself completely. This was too good, too intense, too much.

What if he'd never be the same after all this feeling? What if she changed him and he couldn't find his way back to the comfort of his pain, his grief, which for the past four years had preoccupied and sustained him?

As if sensing his struggle, Darcy bent over him and rubbed her lips over his, half kissing, half talking. 'It's okay, Joe. It's just for tonight.'

Could she sense his struggle? Did she understand his deepest fears? Of course, sex, even sex as wonderful as this, wouldn't change him, couldn't miraculously heal his scars, not that he wanted to be fixed.

What the hell was he doing? He should just enjoy his amazing good fortune and keep his promise to give Darcy way more than she'd given him.

For a few seconds more he allowed her to rock above him, lose herself and take him higher and higher.

Then, set free, he abandoned the fight to only half enjoy this as some form of penance for past crimes and jumped back into the driving seat. He gripped Darcy's hips, guiding her rocking motion, and gritted his teeth against the renewed rush. He flipped them, changing positions as need chewed him up and spat him out. He ran with it, greedy now in his intention to keep his word and keep this about pleasure, with all the feelings she awoke in him locked away.

'Yes, Joe…' she panted as he powered his hips into the cradle of hers '… I'm here with you.' Her fingers bit into his skin as her second climax struck and fuelled his own in a cataclysmic release. When spent he collapsed his weight on top of her, buried his face in her hair and indulged in a prolonged, restorative inhalation of her scent that he never wanted to end.

Then he too burst into laughter and agreed with Darcy's earlier assessment. 'Yep…amazing.'

* * *

Darcy breathed but the air quality seemed off; she couldn't get enough oxygen into her lungs. Joe lay spooned behind her, his sweaty chest stuck to her back, his arms tight around her waist as if he'd never let her go and his breath caressing her shoulder, raising fresh goose bumps. He shifted, quickly disposing of the condom, and then returned to the exact same position, his lips brushing her ear.

'I'm sorry… I'll let you sleep now, I promise.' He pressed a kiss to her neck and Darcy sighed as her libido cracked open one eye, fatigued but still keen.

They hadn't stopped. One round of incredible sex had turned into another and another until, with horrifying inevitability that stung the backs of Darcy's eyes, the first rays of dawn light peeked through the crack in the curtains.

Darcy lay still, scared to move and break the spell. Scared to begin the end of their physical relationship because, despite the deadline, the one night being at her insistence and what she wanted, she couldn't shake the feeling that she'd made some terrible mistake.

Intertwining her fingers with his, she sighed with contentment. She couldn't help it. Joe the lover was a revelation, a game changer. Attentive, tender and commanding, funny and relaxed. A different man, one she could become seriously addicted to if she hadn't made her choice, sworn off relationships, set her priorities.

Joe didn't seem to be in any hurry to release her or sleep himself, so she sank deeper into his embrace for a few more indulgent minutes, lying to herself that they had all the time in the world rather than the hour maximum of reality.

Not even Joe could be ready again so soon, so Darcy took the opportunity to ask the questions she couldn't voice at work.

She stroked her fingertips along his forearm. She wanted to ask about Rosie, how she'd died and why he blamed himself. Instead, she chose what she hoped was the least emotive of her burning questions. 'Why did you and Laura divorce?'

Right about now, after countless orgasms and the most tremendous sexual experience of her life, Darcy rated Joe as a pretty perfect man—smart, dedicated, hard-working and attentive and considerate in bed. She couldn't imagine that he'd cheat. He even put the toilet seat down.

His fingers, which were laced with hers, tensed for a split second. His sigh gusted over the back of her head.

'We tried to stay together after Rosie died.' His voice started off husky like the lover she'd come to learn intimately overnight, but then he cleared his throat as if clearing his mind and shifted at her back. 'At first we grieved together but then, somewhere along the line, something changed. Laura joined a support group and began to share her grief outside of our joint experience.'

Darcy held her breath, aching to hold him, to offer comfort.

'I was glad,' he continued. 'It helped her. She saw that, sadly, we weren't alone in losing a child. She felt consoled to know that we weren't the only ones living the nightmare. That we were one of many families torn apart.'

'And you?' Darcy already anticipated his answer. Because where Laura had seemed to move on, to find love again and embrace the hope of creating a new life, Joe was stuck, punishing himself and living some sort of work-focused half-life.

Not that she could talk… They were similar, she and Joe. Would she too one day regret devoting so much time and energy, so much of herself, to her work instead of finding and treasuring personal happiness?

She felt his body stiffen a fraction, his heart pound a little faster at her back. 'I already knew that we were one of many couples living with loss from my work. The knowledge didn't help me at all. I didn't want to be part of a group with such a hideously unfair shared tragedy. I wanted the impossible.'

'To have Rosie back?' Darcy's voice was barely a whisper now as she crept closer to his deepest pain, feeling as if she had no right. They were just colleagues, temporary lovers. She didn't want more than that, and yet she couldn't ignore his torment or her own desire to know him just a little bit more.

She felt the brisk shake of his head. 'To go back in time.'

Darcy understood. She often regretted the amount of time she'd wasted missing, waiting for and fantasising about her biological father. As if wishing could change things, but it never had. He'd continuously disappointed her and let her down—forgotten birthdays, broken promises, hollow words.

'We started to grieve separately,' Joe said. 'Laura needed my support and I needed nothing, because in my experience nothing made the slightest bit of difference to the pain. The only time I could forget for a few seconds and feel something resembling normal was at the hospital.'

Darcy nodded. She, too, had often patched at the holes in her life with her love of her work—especially after that final rejection from her father and later when she'd broken things off with Dean.

'It was no solace. Feeling normal made me feel guilty, as if I'd forget Rosie without the constant ache of her loss. But I started working later and later anyway, determined to distract myself from the agony gnawing at my insides, even if it was simply from fatigue. At least I felt needed at the hospital. Laura continued searching for her support outside of the marriage and I couldn't blame her. I'd have done the same if I thought anything would stop the pain. We moved in different directions.'

Darcy gripped his fingers tighter, his grief slicing into her like a razor-sharp scalpel. 'I can't imagine what you're feeling, Joe, but I hope that, for your sake, you find something that eases your grief. Perhaps the passage of more time…'

He had so much to offer, the thought of him still alone five years from now made her stomach pinch. But the idea of him with another woman… That made her nauseated, so she forced herself to voice the unthinkable. 'Or when you start dating again, the way Laura has.'

His withdrawal happened swiftly. He rolled away, stood and scrubbed his hands through his hair. 'I know the stages of grief, Darcy.'

'Whoa… I'm sorry.' Darcy sat up and tugged

the covers over her instantly chilly upper body. 'I didn't mean to upset you. I was just trying to help.'

This was why she'd fought her attraction so hard. It was virtually impossible not to feel more, after all they'd been through together.

'I appreciate your sentiments,' he added, his mouth a tight line.

He sounded as if he felt the exact opposite, as if she'd pried too far or knew nothing about his feelings. Yes, she had no personal experience of his level of profound grief, but she was a doctor. She knew that Joe's coping mechanism of choice—to work until numb and punish himself—was in no way a healthy long-term strategy.

Not if he ever wanted to move on.

She knew because spending last night with him had made her realise how empty her own life was. She missed the physical and emotional connection and wanted that in her future. What if she strived and achieved and proved she could make it as a consultant surgeon, only to mourn the things she'd sacrificed, like finding love? Because she'd never truly given her past relationship a proper chance, she saw that now.

Had she ever opened up to Dean the way she had with Joe?

'I didn't mean to overstep the line,' she said,

pushing as she always did. 'I just see that you could have so much more, if only you felt you deserved it.' Surely after the night they'd spent together, after the physical intimacies they'd shared, he'd see that her comments came from a place of caring and a genuine desire to help.

He shook his head and reached for his boxers, tugging them on with abrupt efficiency that told Darcy their lost night of passion was over.

'I know we are putting last night behind us—' if she could '—but that doesn't mean I don't care about you, Joe. Don't you want to find meaning again, to have a second chance at being happy?'

Just like she hoped one day to be. It had to be possible. For both of them.

'Don't doctor me, Darcy.' He jerked on his T-shirt. 'That isn't what this was about. We agreed—just sex.'

Darcy sighed, strangely bereft. He was right. She'd laid down the rules. So why did his emotional withdrawal sting so much? Caring wasn't something you could easily switch off. This was who she was, who she'd fought long and hard to become, despite her own obstacles, her shaky self-belief.

She saw Joe's point of view. 'I don't mean to doctor you, as you put it, but this is how I felt before we slept together and I'm not going to keep my insights to myself if I think it might help you to one day move on.'

Joe shook his head as if in disbelief. 'Maybe this is as good as I'll ever get. I told you I had nothing to offer. Maybe this is as far as I'll move, as much healing as I deserve.'

Darcy's horrified gasp seemed to shock them both. 'You deserve as much as the next person, Joe, as much as Laura.'

And so did she, if she could just stop that fear from holding her back.

'Do I? I put my career before spending time with my family, before my little girl. The day she died I went to work, my head full of other people's illnesses, and I never got to speak to her again.' His eyes hardened and Darcy shivered at how quickly things had turned sour. 'We've both made sacrifices for this job, Darcy, the difference being that I know the high price of those decisions, and it's not a choice I'd make again.'

Darcy swallowed, fighting the irrational fear that he'd just criticised the choice she'd made when she'd picked her career over her relationship. He was in pain. He didn't mean it that way.

Or perhaps, despite the past twenty-four hours, their shared confessions and intimacies, he didn't really understand her after all.

Darcy watched his retreat to the shower, the sense that finally she'd met someone who not only saw her for who she was but valued her, too, deserting her with sickening realisation.

Until he understood himself they'd never see eye to eye, and Darcy was running out of time.

CHAPTER ELEVEN

'MRS O'CONNOR, I understand you're upset but I assure you that we are doing everything we can.' Darcy kept her tone low and reassuring, feeling every scrap of the woman's frustration. 'Your husband's post-op pneumonia is a recognised complication of surgery, especially in someone with his co-morbidities, but we're doing our utmost to help him turn the corner.'

Darcy's temples throbbed. She needed to go home, to leave the sterile hospital environment for a while and recharge her batteries and her reserves. She hated conversations like the one she'd been trapped in for fifteen minutes with this anxious relative, because she was already doing everything she could—for the patient and his family, who'd naturally assumed that he would quickly recover from his routine hernia operation. But sometimes fate had other ideas.

These situations brought up the inevitable conclusion that Darcy's utmost wasn't enough.

Sometimes it couldn't be. With the best will in the world, you couldn't save or cure or even help everyone.

She'd tried to help Joe in Amsterdam after their intimate night, and she'd been knocked back.

'You never explained he might end up here...in Intensive Care.' The woman's pale face haunted Darcy, her pain reminiscent of what she'd witnessed from Joe. This was the worst part of her job and the irrational, vulnerable part of her feared that Joe would side with this relative and blame Darcy too.

They'd left with such a cloud over their relationship as they'd travelled back to London, back to their once more distant and untrusting reality. Darcy knew only one thing for sure: she had no idea what their new dynamic would be and no idea how to untangle her convoluted feelings about the mess they'd made of what should have been a simple one-night stand.

'No one could have predicted the complication,' she said. 'He was moved here so we can monitor him more closely and supplement his breathing with the ventilator. And while it seems alarming, Mr O'Connor is in the best place and receiving the best care.'

Darcy knew that for a fact. She herself had spent the better part of the night checking on her patient and speaking with the ICU team who had taken over management of his care. But she could see nothing she said would make Mrs O'Connor feel reassured.

Darcy couldn't blame the poor woman. She was angry, upset and Darcy had been lashed out at before, more times than she cared to remember. It was part of the job and she always tried not to take it personally. People reacted to stress and grief in different ways. And there was no situation more stressful than a threat to your loved ones.

Look at Joe. Hadn't he too lashed out at Darcy in Amsterdam, snapping closed the lid on his emotions when she'd tried to explore the deepening connection she'd felt after their night together? Understandable after his tragedy. He was protecting himself, the way she tried to avoid her own pain with her pushy, sometimes prickly attitude. She always expected the worst; her father's constant let-downs had conditioned her that way. But a part of her had hoped that she and Joe had moved past shielding and distrust.

Obviously not.

Darcy swallowed down her own hurt.

He'd been inside her, as close as it was physically possible for two people to be, caught her when she'd fallen apart in his arms, their eyes locked. She'd felt so close to him in that second, but it had been an illusion, one she should have known better than to believe.

He didn't want her caring. He didn't want her, and she should be okay with that; after all, she'd been the one to establish the rules.

Through the fog of bitter realisation that she cared too much for Joe, Darcy sensed someone approach. She turned to see the man himself arrive at her side.

An overwhelming sense of relief washed through her. Not relief that he'd wade in and smooth things over with Mrs O'Connor, but a sign of the sustenance she felt in his presence, as if she needed him beyond the physical desire, which if anything had only amplified in the two weeks since Amsterdam.

This. Was. Bad.

She couldn't allow feelings to rule her head, and her head told her to stick to their one-night rule. They certainly seemed to have effortlessly slipped back into their former strained relationship since their return.

'Ms Wright.' Joe cast her a brief look—long enough for Darcy's silly heart to pound and for her to see that he, too, appeared to share her fatigue if the fine lines and dark shadows around his beautiful eyes were any indication. Perhaps he was having trouble sleeping since the conference, just like her.

No, he probably slept like a baby knowing his emotions were safely locked down, out of harm's way. Knowing she'd soon be gone and he could resume, unscathed, his solitary, self-inflicted prison sentence.

'Mrs O'Connor, I'm Joe Austin, your husband's consultant.' He shook the woman's hand and reached for the observation chart, which would tell him that their patient was seriously unwell but, for now, stable.

'Good to finally meet you,' Mrs O'Connor said, her tone brisk with recrimination.

Darcy held her breath, waiting for what came next. She'd experienced this before. Patients often felt they weren't receiving top notch care unless the consultant themselves undertook every aspect of their treatment. But Joe was only one man—he couldn't possibly be in all places at once, operating and in clinic and there on the wards to administer every dose of antibiotics and perform every blood test.

He probably wished he could be. Then he could keep busy enough to distract himself and keep running from life. Did he fear that the memory of Rosie might slip out of his grasp if he allowed himself to be happy?

Couldn't he see that he carried her with him inside, safe and secure and permanent?

He'd made it clear that Darcy had no place in pointing out any of this.

'Yes, Ms Wright and I are incredibly disappointed that your husband's routine operation has resulted in a post-operative chest infection. Understandably, you are very worried.' Joe's quiet tone rang with calm authority. Unlike when they'd first met, when this had rubbed her up the wrong way, Darcy hoped Mrs O'Connor felt its soothing power, just as she did.

At least he still referred to them as a team, even if he no longer felt that they were one.

'Well…' Mrs O'Connor's anger deflated a little now that Joe, the big boss, was here simply repeating all the assurances Darcy had already made. 'I'm sure you'll do everything you can to get him well again.'

Darcy bit her tongue, pretending she didn't exist. If a relative felt comfort from hearing things from the horse's mouth, she couldn't complain. If only it didn't make her feel written out of the equation.

But perhaps her confusion over Joe and where they stood was more to blame. In Amsterdam she'd felt valued and accepted, but that was before he'd rejected her compassion and care. Now she was back to guessing his opinions.

Joe subtly stepped closer to Darcy, bringing her back into Mrs O'Connor's line of sight. 'Ms

Wright and the intensive care staff have acted quickly in transferring Mr O'Connor here. He's in the right place, with an amazing team of doctors and nurses to care for him. Be assured we will continue to do everything we can to treat his pneumonia. From a surgical standpoint, Ms Wright informed me that his operation ran smoothly and that his scar is healing beautifully.'

Darcy unfurled under his praise like a flower in the sun. At least outwardly he supported her and her management of Mr O'Connor.

Joe's acknowledgement shouldn't matter, but it reminded her what she already knew: she *was* good enough to work for him. She was his equal. But did his professional consideration on top of their growing intimacy prove that somewhere, beneath his grief and pain and guilt, he cared about her, just as she'd begun to care about him?

Joe's magic touch worked on Mrs O'Connor, too. While Darcy tried to still the rampaging of her foolish heart that seemed to want impossible things, the other woman cast a small relieved smile in Darcy's direction before turning her attention on Joe once more. 'Yes… So will you be coming back to check on him later?'

'I'll check in tomorrow, but in the meantime I have the utmost faith in the medical team on ICU and in Ms Wright, who takes excellent care of all of my patients.'

Darcy swallowed convulsively, her reaction telling her how invested she'd become in Joe and how close to the surface her feelings lurked. Close enough that she could be seriously hurt.

She couldn't be falling for him. She refused to allow it.

Mrs O'Connor cast Darcy one last speculative look and hurried back to her husband's bedside.

Awkwardness descended, cloaking Darcy in its icy tentacles. She didn't want to look at Joe in case it confirmed all of her worst fears—that, despite her best intentions, she was in too deep.

'Shall we continue the rest of the round back on the surgical ward?' Joe looked down at her with an expectant expression, no hint that he in any way struggled with the post-sex boundaries they'd imposed in Amsterdam, when all Darcy wanted to do was either rip off his clothes or force him to let her in, emotionally. Preferably both.

No, no, no…

Darcy nodded woodenly, her head a mess. Every step back towards the surgical wing of the hospital along the sunlit corridor might as well have been on broken glass, so stilted and uncomfortable was the atmosphere. Eventually, Darcy couldn't stand the silence.

'Thanks for smoothing that over,' she said.

'I hope she wasn't too rude to you,' said Joe.

'It's hard to stay objective and calm when your loved one's fate is uncertain.'

'Of course.' Darcy glanced over at his stoic profile, knowing he must be thinking about Rosie. Unable to read him, she wished she could simply pull his X-ray and blood work and know exactly what he felt inside.

But maybe she didn't want to know. Maybe it would only confirm she was alone in wanting more than that one night. She sighed; she couldn't face another slap of rejection.

'Don't take it to heart,' he said. 'Sometimes patients and relatives need to know where the buck stops. It will stop with you soon enough, when you move on from City.' He paused outside the surgical ward and faced her. 'By the way, I forwarded the reference you asked for to Manchester Hospital. When is your interview?'

He gave so little away. Where had all that openness, the easy non-verbal communication between them gone?

'Next week.' Darcy's stomach cramped. His reminder that she'd soon take up a post in another hospital, which could be anywhere in the country, amplified the panic fluttering in her chest. She'd likely never see Joe again. Well, perhaps at a surgical conference in the future. Would they both still be single? Would they hook up for old times' sake? Would that be enough?

Five weeks ago that scenario might have sat comfortably with her, but now she found the idea of casual sex, even if it was with Joe, depressing. She wanted more; she wanted it all—her career and a meaningful private life—and for a moment in his arms that had seemed possible.

She imagined bumping into him down the track, seeing him happy, a shiny new wedding ring on his finger. Inexplicable emotion gripped Darcy's throat so her words emerged strangled. 'Thanks…for the reference.'

She thought back to her first day, when a letter of endorsement had been all she'd wanted from Joe. Now her wants were so much more…complex. Impractical and terrifying.

'All part of my job,' he said, pushing open the door to the ward and stepping aside for Darcy to pass.

Yes, that was all she was to him—work, a colleague. He'd warned her there was no room inside him for anything else and she'd believed, hoped, that one night would be enough.

Only now…

Joe paused just inside the ward and levelled his stare on Darcy, the intense, soul-searching one she'd grown to expect during their long sleepless night in an Amsterdam hotel. Despite their location, her own warnings and plain old common sense, which demanded she not over-interpret that look, her pulse flew, buzzing in her ears, the danger deafening.

Careful…

'We should talk,' he said, 'before the ward round.'

There was a utility room at the entrance to the ward. Before she could argue or agree, Joe glanced toward the empty nurses' station and then gripped Darcy's arm and ushered her inside.

Darcy backed up into the small room, lost for words. Her heart hammered against her ribs, which was silly because he wasn't likely to pounce on her and rip off her clothes in a room regularly entered by ward staff. So why did she suddenly wish the door had a lock?

He paced close, his stare intent. The appearance of an urbane professional man slipped away, replaced by the look of a hungry predator. Darcy shivered. Her reaction to this unexpected diversion confirmed what she already knew. Despite the danger, she craved more than the night they'd shared, more than to be a part of his work, a colleague. More of them together.

Could he want the same?

'What are you doing?' she asked, her voice wobbling with anticipation.

Please let him be about to kiss her.

'This.' In two swift strides Joe closed the distance. He scooped one strong arm around her waist and, with a triumphant grunt, slammed his mouth over hers in a frantic kiss that answered every one of Darcy's unspoken prayers.

Feeling as if she were levitating, she parted her lips, her tongue meeting his, duelling, thrusting, devouring. This was what she'd missed since Amsterdam. It was reckless and perilous and alarming, but she could no more resist than she could switch off her feelings.

They broke for air, Joe's lips continuing a trail of kisses over her jaw towards her earlobe.

'What are we doing?' panted Darcy, curling her fingers into his hair and tugging at the lapel of his suit jacket, bringing him closer and dragging his lips back for another kiss.

'Taking a big risk, but I don't care.' He crowded her back against the counter, his big body trapping her exactly where she wanted to be.

'I can't stop thinking about you,' he said, his words muffled against her skin. 'Every time we've seen each other I've had to stop myself from touching you, reaching for your hand, kissing you. I almost broke on ICU and dragged you into my arms.'

Joe's thigh pushed between her legs. 'I brought you in here to apologise for the way I reacted in Amsterdam. But I can't seem to keep my hands off you.' He gripped her waist, hoisting her backside up onto the table. Darcy closed her eyes, lost to physical sensation as Joe snaked his hand around her waist and trailed his voracious lips down the side of her neck.

She should curtail this. Anyone could come in at any second. She was certain that fornicating in a storage cupboard was a sackable offence, but she just couldn't bring herself to care enough, already lost under the hypnotic spell of the way Joe made her feel.

As if, with the right man, she could have it all. She could feel whole for the first time in her life. But Joe couldn't be the right man. He wasn't ready to forgive himself. His determination to be alone put Darcy in a highly risky position. She'd been the one to make all of the concessions, all of the sacrifices in the past. She'd done it with her father growing up—holding out hope that they'd resume the closeness they'd shared in those first few years, forgiving him when his broken promises broke her heart, over and over, keeping a distance from Grant in case it provoked her father's disappointment—and also with Dean out of ingrained habit.

But with Joe she was in deeper water.

'We said we wouldn't do this again,' she said, hooking her fingers through the belt loops of his trousers so he couldn't escape. 'You said you kept your promises.'

Was that her desperately breathy voice goading him to ignore the rules they'd agreed on and be exactly what she needed?

Please let him break this promise...

'I never promised to stop wanting you, to stop craving you,' he said, the words pressed against her skin as he kissed a delirious path from the vee of chest her top exposed to the angle of her jaw.

'Don't stop,' she said as his tongue flicked at the lobe of her ear. They couldn't have sex in the utility room at the hospital, but perhaps there was little harm in continuing this relationship until she left City. It was only a handful of weeks, a nice tidy deadline she had time to get used to.

But could she ever get used to the way he made her feel?

He pulled away enough to pin her with his sexy stare. 'Are you free tonight?' Joe cupped her breast and rubbed her nipple through her layers of clothing.

She bucked against him, her body incinerating at his touch and all the erotic memories it evoked. Not fair.

'Um...' She wanted to ask, *Free for what?* To cover an extra shift, a date, more sex? Despite the warning exhilaration rendering her virtually speechless, she was definitely ready and willing for the latter two.

'I'm sorry...for the way things ended in Amsterdam.' His gruff voice, his warm breath on her neck, did things to her willpower. 'I hoped you might allow me to make it up to you…' his other hand slipped under the hem of her top until he brushed bare flesh; her body sprang alive, like the jolt from a defibrillator '…with dinner.'

No, say no.

'Um…' Were there no words left in her vocabulary? Had she become a gibbering wreck of hormones and emotions, too addicted to Joe to make any sense?

He cupped her cheek, swiped the pad of his thumb over her bottom lip, sincerity and that hint of vulnerability in his beautiful eyes. 'We could go out to a restaurant if you want, or I could cook. I only live two Tube stops away from here.' He pressed his hips forward between her legs and her body melted, all fight draining away until she was left with only need and feelings.

Feelings that erred perilously close to the edge of the fall.

No, she couldn't. She mustn't.

'Okay…' Darcy sighed, helpless to resist as his tempting kisses resumed.

Uninhibited by the way he made her feel complete, she slipped one hand under his suit jacket and around his waist, her fingertips tracing the muscles of his back through his shirt. Her other hand found the hard length of him behind the zip of his trousers and they groaned together.

Darcy closed her eyes against the spiralling sensations he effortlessly created. Could she wait until tonight? She dropped her head back, exposed her neck to his mouth in utter surrender.

With a thud, the back of her head hit the shelving that lined the wall behind. A cacophony of packages—syringes, gauze, catheter tubes—rained down on them like medical confetti.

It broke the tension. Darcy laughed, clapped her hand over her mouth. Joe rested his forehead against hers and chuckled, the fraught arousal draining from his features.

'Perfect timing,' he said, pressing one last kiss to her lips. He helped Darcy slide from the counter and speared his hand through his hair, trying to make himself presentable once more.

Her heart clenched. He looked so sexy she was certain she wouldn't have stopped without the interruption. Was she so far gone that she'd forget where they were, forget that they'd both sworn off relationships and this had no long-term future?

They righted their clothing and picked up the fallen equipment, shoved it into the correct cubby on the wall, their matching knowing smiles infectious.

'So...' Joe said, 'meet me at six, my office?' The excitement lingering in his eyes called to the part of Darcy that was now full-blown addicted to Joe Austin. For her self-preservation, to protect that last part of her heart, she needed to know how he saw this panning out.

'So, will it be like a date?' she croaked, chiding herself for the hope that bloomed inside.

He shrugged, a moment's hesitation confirming that he too was in uncharted territory. 'If you like. After all, you'll soon be moving on. I need to get my fill of your company before you leave.'

That he wanted more, just like her, terrified and elated her. That he'd, too, identified a natural and convenient deadline should reassure her. But she no longer wanted just sex; she craved their emotional connection, the depth of which she'd never before experienced. Could she take more incredible sex without needing him to open up emotionally? Could she protect herself if he once again shut her out?

She trembled, her nerves frayed. One thing was evident; she couldn't risk falling all the way in love with a man incapable of giving her what she needed. She couldn't be second best or an afterthought or good enough. Next time she committed to a man she wanted to be everything to him, his world.

'Okay, a date it is.' Darcy nodded, her heart fluttering wildly. While good, her diagnostic skills struggled to determine the cause of her palpitations. The euphoria she craved or trepidation for the rejection she expected?

Only time would tell the outcome for her and Joe.

CHAPTER TWELVE

JOE PLACED A bowl of steaming pasta in front of Darcy and refilled her wine glass before taking his seat opposite. Lightness rose in his chest. It was good to have her all to himself, in his home. No demons, no pressure, no expectation.

Just the constant and undeniable need to be with her, talk to her, touch her.

His growing obsession was understandable after being alone for so long. And he'd convinced himself that there was little risk; she'd soon be moving on.

But…

He couldn't seem to shake the hollow dread that settled in the pit of his stomach when he imagined the end of this.

Darcy leaned over the dish and inhaled the fragrant steam and then offered him an impressed smile that warmed the coldest recesses of his soul. 'This smells delicious. Thank you.'

'It's just pasta…' He wished he had more to

offer her than a simple home-cooked meal. She deserved champagne and caviar, satin sheets and a whirlwind romance.

She shrugged. 'No one's ever really cooked for me before.' She took a sip of wine and picked up her fork, her eyes alight with reflections from the candles.

'Really?' Joe hid his surprise. 'Not even your ex?' He frowned. What sort of a man would propose to Darcy and then allow her to escape?

Darcy swallowed the mouthful, her eyes darting away from Joe's. 'No...' She bit her lip as if choosing her words carefully. 'Dean was...an artist. The practicalities of everyday life—cooking, shopping, paying the bills—often passed him by while he worked.'

Joe's irritation flickered to life on Darcy's behalf. Laura and Joe had shared the household responsibilities. Working from home was still working. The idea of Darcy returning home after a long gruelling day at the hospital with no support or understanding left him itching with exasperation.

'Did you live together?' he asked, trying to picture the driven, ambitious woman he knew in a serious relationship. 'I can't imagine you happily working a sixty-hour week *and* doing all of the household chores.' Nor should she have to.

This wasn't the Dark Ages. Her career was just as important as Joe's.

Darcy looked uncomfortable but then, with a small sigh, dropped her guard. He hadn't realised how much he'd held out for the return of their confidences, how he craved her trust as strongly as he craved her lips.

'We did live together,' she said. 'Divvying up the everyday tasks became a bone of contention. Among others.'

Joe raised his eyebrow in enquiry. Relaxed by the wine and the soft music he'd selected, Darcy seemed to be in a confessional mood that lessened Joe's guilt for pushing her away after they'd slept together. Their night had shocked him, not only the violence of his insatiable physical desire for Darcy, but also because he wanted more, wanted to know every fine internal intricacy of her mind.

Like why she was still unattached. It seemed preposterous that she hadn't been snapped up when she was most guys' dream woman.

'He never really understood my career. Our career.' Darcy twirled her wine glass by the stem, watching the deep red liquid catch the light as she talked about her ex. 'He thought such a utilitarian job should keep regular hours.' She rested her elbows on the table and sought Joe's eyes. 'We had ups and downs like any couple. He'd complain if I was late to one of his gallery exhibitions or if I couldn't socialise with his friends because of my on-call commitments. I guess he never really understood me either, or my drive.'

A surge of protective feelings welled up in Joe. 'It's a common point of friction between doctors and their non-medical spouses.' He and Laura had had their fair share of trials and tribulations. Darcy deserved a partner who appreciated her qualities.

'So you called it off?' he asked, although she'd already admitted this. But he wanted to know why. He wanted to know if Darcy's heart had been broken by this man who'd made her doubt herself, made her choose.

'I did,' she said, meeting Joe's gaze. 'I'm not saying I was perfect. At times, I might have acted as if my job was more important than his… I've always been ambitious. I guess I needed to prove to myself that I could be and do anything after growing up with so much…rejection. He asked me to marry him, and initially I said yes, but the minute the word left my mouth it felt like the wrong decision.'

Joe tried not to give rein to the envy that she'd almost married this guy. 'Why was it the wrong decision? Don't you want to get married one day?' Now why the hell had he asked that? What business was it of his? Except he cared about her and wanted her to be happy. She deserved to have it all one day, as he had.

She swallowed, her eyes brimming with vulnerability. 'I felt like he'd never fully accept me for who I am—my motivations and values. I'd already sacrificed so much of myself trying to be the kind of daughter that my father would want, not that I knew then what would make him want to stay around. For a long time I made myself feel like an outsider in my own family. I never knew when he'd reappear, so it was as if I felt the need to keep a part of myself constantly ready for him to show up and whisk me away for a one-on-one. I was a child. I guess I thought I couldn't have both. Now I see that I was emotionally withdrawing from the people who loved me the most, Grant, my sisters to a degree, even my mother. Because I tried to hide some of my disappointment when he let me down for the times my father would return. I didn't want her to be angry with him on my behalf. It took most of my late teens and early twenties to untangle those childhood beliefs and embrace my family one hundred per cent.'

Joe nodded, new respect for her strength and determination making his breathing tight.

'With Dean,' she continued, 'it felt as if one day I'd have to choose again, sacrifice our relationship or my job.' She shrugged. 'I knew there was no contest, so I called it off before either of us could get hurt.'

Joe sensed there was more to the story, more to her motivation. Most people successfully combined a career and a personal life. Darcy's polarised view smacked of self-preservation, fear. No one understood that better than Joe. 'So you pulled the plug pre-emptively, before giving commitment a try?'

Her eyes flashed to his, a flare of defensiveness, then resignation. 'Yes… I suppose I did. I wanted to save myself the emotional fallout when our relationship broke down, as it eventually would. I guess I didn't love him enough to take that chance.'

Unease prickled along Joe's spine. It shouldn't matter to him that she, too, had relationship reservations. Why was he pushing this? He wanted to be with her, to take as much of her as she'd give him in the time they had left, not dissect her past choices to determine where he would fit into her life. He wasn't offering her long-term, so why did it bother him that she'd shied away from committing to another man?

'It might have lasted,' said Joe, playing devil's advocate even as his blood pumped harder, knowing that Darcy hadn't loved this man from her past enough. 'None of us can predict the future,' he said. 'No one knows what awaits us around the bend. If we did, maybe we'd never do anything. Never grow or thrive or experience wondrous joy.'

Her eyes softened. She was thinking about him and Rosie, he could tell. Yes, Joe had first-hand experience of life's highs and lows and fickleness.

'I guess I was scared,' she said, her voice breaking.

Joe held his breath, desperate to hold her but needing to complete the Darcy puzzle, too. She was opening all the way up to him and his greedy, selfish side craved everything she was willing to give. Perhaps talking about her past would help her, the way telling her small things about Rosie had helped him. When she left City he'd sleep better at night knowing that he'd done everything in his power to support her onward journey, as a clinician and as a person.

'I did hold back from Dean, from full commitment.' Her candour, her bravery mesmerised him. 'I thought our differences, which at times seemed insurmountable, would push us apart eventually.' She shrugged, her small smile shifting something inside Joe.

'So you pushed first, to protect yourself.' His voice was low, coaxing, pleading for her to share this part of herself that she normally guarded. He was in no way judging. Humans were at their most unpredictable and complex when frightened or in pain. 'It's understandable after what you went through growing up.'

Her father's abandonment, his repeated rejection, would have affected bright, emotionally intelligent Darcy. The feeling of being somehow unworthy of his love might have eased the more she pushed herself academically and later in her work as a doctor, but the belief would ultimately hold her back from deep connections with others, from true contentment.

He knew. He'd deliberately withdrawn and avoided developing bonds since he'd lost Rosie, but he wanted more than that for Darcy.

She shrugged, her colour high. She was intuitive enough to read between the lines. He'd hit the nail on the head.

The thought depressed him more than it should. It wasn't his place to fix her, not when he'd promised her nothing beyond a few more nights of incredible sex. Except he couldn't stop himself, just as he'd been powerless to deny his urges in the utility room earlier.

'What about you?' she asked, turning the tables. 'Do you think you'll ever want another shot at happiness?' Doubt flashed in her eyes, brief and unfamiliar. Did she imagine more between them?

Joe's stomach pinched with unease. 'Ah... I've

already experienced love *and* its flipside. At first it feels great, you feel invincible, but then…' He swallowed his own fears gripping his throat. 'I never want to feel that degree of pain again.' He looked away from her searching stare, his resolve hardening. 'It's not for everyone, but I'm happy with my lonely, risk-free existence.'

He couldn't bear to see the emotions in Darcy's eyes. Sorrow for him, perhaps disappointment that he wasn't just like her, pushing for the best outcome, to be the best version of himself.

How he wished he could be different, open to exploring this connection with Darcy beyond a few passionate nights. A part of him would love to be the kind of man she deserved, the kind who would love her unconditionally and chase away all of her doubts about her worth. But he'd been there before, and nothing he'd done could stop it all slipping through his fingers.

Already he felt his insatiable need for Darcy had begun to dictate his emotional happiness. When she smiled it elevated his mood. If she challenged him he felt enlivened, cheerful, animated. And when she returned his kisses, her passion burning as brightly as his own, he became convinced that *anything* was possible.

But that was a lie. He couldn't rely on another person to that degree.

'I guess we're similar in avoiding risky emotional fallout,' she said, and Joe's skin crawled with unfamiliar dejection. Maybe they were too similar—Darcy and the old Joe. The man he'd been before he was forced to realise that without your loved ones there was no one to strive for. What would stop Darcy pushing away the next man who got too close?

She settled those defiant and determined eyes on his. 'Dean wasn't the one for me. I'm glad that I chose to focus on myself instead of investing valuable time and energy on the wrong priority.' She lifted her chin and Joe saw the flicker of fear behind her bravado.

Wasn't that how he felt about his job and all the missed chances to spend time with the most valuable people in the world: family?

Joe reached out and took her hand, needing her touch to remind himself that their physical connection had to be enough. 'Good for you.'

He didn't want more than this, but to hear her fear, how she ran from commitment, reminded him that waking up from the past grief-dulled four years, embracing something life-enhancing and passionate with this woman, was one thing. But chancing more than that when there were no guarantees in life and Darcy, for all her amazing qualities, had been a flight risk in the past… That seemed unthinkable.

* * *

Darcy accepted another glass of wine and made room for Joe on the sofa, her emotions conflicted. She'd been warmed by his attentiveness, touched by his cooking and even welcomed his gentle enquiries. They finally had a chance to be alone and explore each other on a deeper level and it felt good to open up to him. She trusted him.

But a niggle of unease permeated her relaxed, hopeful mood.

Joe understood her past fear of commitment because it was something they had in common, for different reasons. Only, for the first time in her life, Darcy glimpsed a way forward, the possibility of having it all. With Joe. If only he could meet her halfway along the same path.

But no matter how hard she tried to imagine a future where she could have everything—a relationship with a man who understood and supported her and a career she found fulfilling—she always circled back to the same roadblock: Joe's grief.

She saw shadows of it whenever she looked into his deep brown eyes. He was trapped by it, scared to let go in case he lost the memories, lost more of his little girl than he had already.

And she couldn't blame him for clinging to the one thing he felt connected him to Rosie. She'd do the same.

Except she wanted more for him than half a life, which was tinged with so much sadness. She wanted him to be the wonderful man he was and to find self-forgiveness.

She took his hand, curled her fingers into his palm. They looked down at their entwined hands. Darcy's pulse throbbed to the tips of her fingers at the thrill and decadence of Joe's touch.

'Tell me about Rosie,' Darcy whispered. 'I'd love to have met her.' Her enquiry was long overdue, but there was never the right time for such an emotive conversation at the hospital, and until recently she'd been too unsure of Joe's emotional shield to ask. Even now, when they'd spent an evening learning new things about the other, warning signs flashed in her mind. He'd withdrawn in Amsterdam. Would tonight end with a repeat? Him defensive and her pushing him further away?

Joe's breath shuddered out on a slow exhale. He stared at the flickering candle flame on the coffee table, lost in his thoughts. 'She was the sweetest little girl. So precious, as all children are. I adored her.' Their stares connected and Darcy was crushed by the outpouring of stark emotions she saw.

She smiled, steering him away from Rosie's final minutes, the mechanics of which only appeased her doctor's curiosity. She cared much more about Joe's recovery. 'What was your favourite thing to do together?'

Darcy's heart banged against her ribs. The urge to hold Joe in her arms and never let him go, to always be there for him in whatever capacity he'd allow, was almost overwhelming. She realised way too late that where Joe was concerned she seemed to have forgotten her suit of armour.

He smiled, remembering, and her spirit soared. 'We would cook breakfast together on the weekend. Her favourite—pancakes with banana and maple syrup.' He talked with his hands, so Darcy could vividly picture the scene. 'We'd trash the kitchen and then eat the results, but we always needed a story before tackling the washing-up. My girl was a bookworm.' Pride warmed his expression. 'She loved it when I read to her.'

Darcy struggled to speak past her choked throat. 'What a beautiful memory, Joe.' She cupped his face and stroked her thumb over his stubble-rough jaw. 'Your relationship sounds so close. You were both so lucky to have each other.'

Joe stared, nodded, his eyes full of love for his daughter and sympathy for Darcy. 'Yes, we were. She was a gift. I miss her so much.'

Joe's love for his daughter, the simple but special moments he described, amplified Darcy's own sense of loss for something she'd never had—that one person to share everything with.

To build a life, a family, love. She wrapped her arms around Joe's shoulders and held him close, more for her own comfort than his.

'It would have been her tenth birthday next week,' he said, gripping Darcy with equal compulsion, the thump of his heart against hers sure and steadfast. 'I try to imagine how she would look, how she'd have changed as she grew, who she'd resemble most, me or Laura.'

Darcy glanced around the room, spying only one or two framed photos of them together on the mantelpiece. No wonder he was lonely here, with his sparse reminders. He clearly thought about Rosie all the time, but where the family home she'd visited in Surrey, the home he'd left to Laura after their split, was alive with the presence of their daughter, Joe's house, but for those two framed photos, resembled more of a bachelor pad.

She pulled back to look into his face. She cherished his trust. 'Will you celebrate the day?'

He frowned as if she'd suggested something he'd never considered. 'Last year Laura and I visited Rosie's grave and took toys and flowers, but this year…' he swallowed, clearly struggling '… I suspect she'll want to go alone, with Phil.'

Darcy's soul ached anew. She wanted to volunteer to go with him, to be whatever he needed in his time of grief and remembrance. But he'd never accept that from her. She wasn't his partner. She wasn't even his girlfriend.

To keep her mouth shut and her offer to herself, she leaned forward and kissed his temple. She couldn't stop herself from touching him, comforting him, connecting.

'Why don't you have a party—make a stack of Rosie's favourite pancakes and decorate them with ten candles?'

He frowned and Darcy worried that he'd see her suggestion as interference.

'I'm sorry, Joe. I don't mean to upset you. I can only imagine how you must feel. But it's okay to learn to live with your wonderful memories of Rosie in a different way. It's natural for a parent-child relationship to change with time. It won't mean that you love her any less because you smile.'

Joe scrunched his eyes closed and dropped his forehead to hers. He was silent for so long Darcy squirmed that she'd overstepped the line and ruined their evening.

Then he drew back, a small frown between his brows. 'When did you last reconnect with your biological father?'

Darcy stiffened, withdrawing from the pain still potent enough to sting. A part of her wanted to protect her deepest shame, that for her father she hadn't been good enough, but Joe had shared so much with her. She wanted him to know that he wasn't alone with his regrets. She had them too.

'I looked him up when I started medical school,' she said, the humiliating memories flooding back. 'I hadn't seen him for years. Part of me hoped that he'd want a relationship with the adult me. I wanted to show him that I was someone he could be proud of. I was going to be a doctor and, thanks to that show I participated in, I was going to be on TV.'

She shook her head at her naiveté, struggling to finish the story because it brought out all of her most painful insecurities—the last thing she wanted with Joe, the man she was falling for. 'He invited me to his home—he'd moved to Scotland. I almost threw up on the train journey; I was so nervous and excited and hopeful.'

Joe cupped her cheek and pressed his lips to her forehead, anticipating the *but*. She fell a little harder in that moment, grateful that he understood her so intuitively. Grateful for his strength.

'I arrived to find that he'd remarried. He had two new daughters, one six and one a year old, the age I was when he first took off. It was hard to see how much he adored his girls.'

She blinked away the sting of tears. 'I felt betrayed—it wasn't that he didn't want children; he just didn't want *me*. The visit was a disaster.

I couldn't hide my anger, my…disappointment. I lashed out at him with some home truths and haven't seen him since.'

Air rushed from her lungs on a cathartic exhale. The only other people she'd told the details of that story to were Stella and Lily.

'I'm so sorry.' Joe held her close, his heart thudding against hers in solidarity. It felt like all she'd ever need to tackle life's future obstacles. But the bitter taste in the back of her throat reminded her that she couldn't rely on Joe. As wonderful as he was, Joe wasn't ready to be the man for her.

'It's okay.' She sniffed, put on her brave face. 'It was good for me in a way. I started taking myself more seriously, stared knuckling down even more with my studies and planning my future. It gave me renewed purpose, the work ethic I still have today. Perhaps I wouldn't have even become a doctor if he'd accepted me with open arms.'

Joe pulled back to look at her, his thumb caressing her cheek where he still cupped her face. 'Of course you would. You're an innate healer. You were always going to be the gifted surgeon you are now. You were always destined to be your amazing self. Don't give him credit he doesn't deserve when your success, your inspiring qualities, are down to you and you alone.'

He brushed his lips over Darcy's in a whisper of a kiss. 'Sometimes it's easier for people to move on and try to forget their past mistakes. Staying with them and working for redemption is harder, takes more self-reflection and honesty. Humans are essentially lazy cowards who avoid pain at all costs.'

Darcy understood that he referred to her father, but instinctively knew that Joe's condemnation also included himself. She gripped both of his hands, demanding his attention.

'Joe, you didn't do anything wrong. You are an incredible man.' She pressed her hand to her breastbone. 'I know in here, deep down in my soul, that Rosie would be so proud of her dad. I know because the little girl I was, the one so desperate for her real father to care, would have done anything for a father like you.'

His tight swallow told her anything he might want to say was trapped in his throat. She hated the remaining distance between them so she leaned in and pressed her lips to his, seeking and giving refuge. He took her kiss as if reaching for a lifeline, his arms clutching her so tight she felt melded to his chest as if they were one.

His mouth grew demanding, overpowering and yielding in perfect harmony so that Darcy forgot her own pain, forgot that Joe might not want her consolation, forgot every doubt as she lost herself in their kiss.

Comfort quickly turned to passion. Darcy tugged at Joe's shirt and he unclasped her bra with one hand. Tearing his mouth from hers, he stood and lifted her into his arms.

'I want you. I've been in hell since Amsterdam.' He strode towards what she assumed was his bedroom and kicked open the door.

She'd missed her chance to slam on the brakes, reconstruct some semblance of a barrier against her feelings for Joe. They'd spilled free the minute he'd begun to confide in her, talking about his daughter, and it was too late to scoop them all up now.

She was in too deep.

'Joe, hurry,' Darcy cried as they stripped, tossed clothes away with furious impatience. As they finally found each other completely naked, skin to warm skin, their groans resounded in unison around the darkened bedroom.

Darcy knew she was making a mistake because nothing had ever felt this good, or this important. It had to be bad. It had to mean that rejection wasn't far away. She shouldn't trust it.

Except she wanted to be wrong. She wanted Joe to declare himself ready to open his emotional vault. She wanted to trust him with her heart, the way she'd never trusted before. She wanted them to face this scary new future together, as much a team as a couple, as they were at work.

When he covered himself in protection and pushed inside her she had to dig her teeth into his shoulder to stop her tears. It was too good. They were too in sync, the enormity of her feelings for this man bursting forth as she shattered around him and clung on for dear life.

Joe crushed her, spent, and then rolled to the side, taking her with him, clinging, holding, stroking as if he'd never let her go. Darcy lay in the circle of his strong arms, her cheek pressed against his slowing heart, too scared to breathe, because if she'd thought she was terrified that he'd somehow let her down, how on earth would she ever survive falling in love?

CHAPTER THIRTEEN

DARCY FLUNG OPEN her front door to find a sight for sore eyes standing on her doorstep: Joe. His dazzling smile knocked the wind from her lungs. The familiar hint of sadness around his eyes made her feel needed. That he'd come to her on this day, Rosie's birthday, a sure sign of his personal feelings.

He must care.

Her heart leapt into her throat and she threw her arms around him, pressing a kiss to his neck. 'What are you doing here? I literally just arrived home from Manchester.' She hadn't even had time to change out of her interview suit after spending the day touting her skills as a candidate for the newest general surgeon consultant post on offer.

'I wanted to see you.' He kissed her long and deep, and Darcy forgot how to breathe. How could she have missed him so profoundly? She'd only been away one night. How would she survive working three hundred miles away when her body felt starved of him after only twenty-four hours?

When they broke apart she invited him in and closed the door.

'How was the interview?' he asked, placing the shopping bag he carried at his feet to shrug out of his jacket.

For the first time since she'd opened the door to find him expectantly seeking her out, the nauseating taste of failure returned. 'It seemed to go well.' She looked at her feet, which were bare and still protesting the heels she'd worn for her interview. 'The panel were friendly and interested in my past research, but…'

She glanced up at Joe, knowing he'd understand what today's failure meant to Darcy.

'But you didn't get the job?' He looked disappointed, gutted on her behalf, tired.

The mean little doubts that had plagued her on the train journey home—that perhaps his reference hadn't been the glowing endorsement she'd needed to secure the job—now seemed trivial and disloyal. Perhaps her thoughts had been a desperate diversion from ruminating on her feelings, because Darcy was more certain than ever that she was falling deeply in love.

Stupid, foolish woman.

'No. They chose the guy from Scotland, the

one with a PhD and a large portfolio of research.' Darcy hung Joe's coat on the rack in the hallway and led him into the living room, where Stella lounged on the sofa after her shift at the hospital.

'Joe, this is my sister, Stella. Stella, this is Joe Austin, my consultant.' Darcy winced inside. She wanted to be able to introduce him in another more personal way but, regardless of her feelings, the fantasies she'd allowed herself to concoct—that he'd realise he couldn't live without her, beg her to stay in London and ask her to move in with him—that was all he was to her in reality.

Stella flushed as she uncurled herself from the sofa and shook Joe's hand. 'I know who he is.' She rolled her eyes at Darcy and then to Joe said, 'Nice to meet you. I…uh… I was just about to go for a run so I'll… um…leave you two to it.'

With all the subtlety of a baby rhinoceros, Stella jogged upstairs to change.

Darcy bit her lip and searched Joe's face for signs that he was upset by her sister's obvious assumption. 'Sorry. She's figured out we're sleeping together. You can't hide anything from sisters!' And, of course, Darcy had in turn questioned Stella about Aaron's cryptic reaction to her name. 'But she's the soul of discretion, I promise.' She didn't want him to feel uncomfortable if he ran into Stella at the hospital after Darcy left.

'I'm not worried.' His apparent ease rankled.

Perhaps he wouldn't even miss her. Perhaps he'd move on, too, seek physical comfort from his next registrar.

'Have you eaten?' He held his shopping bag aloft.

Darcy chided herself for her irrational hope and her pointless jealousy. 'No—are you cooking?' How could she resist any part of him? She'd take whatever he was willing to give her until she left, and somehow try to get over him from afar.

Hopefully she'd be too busy working to give him a second thought.

Joe nodded, tugging her back in for another kiss that felt loaded with all the unspoken confidences and confessions Darcy wanted to hear.

I'm falling for you.

I don't want you to move so far away.

I'm ready to give us a try.

'Today's the day,' he said, sliding his hand under Darcy's jacket to stroke her back.

She nodded, pressing kisses to his face in order to chase away the shadows haunting his expression and her own desire to blurt out her feelings. 'I know. Joe… I'm so touched that you called around.'

Surely the fact that he'd come to her, of all people, meant that he cared more than he'd expressed. That a part of him already considered them more than a casual, sex-only fling.

'I brought steaks and salad.' His open smile faltered. 'And pancake mix... I thought we could...celebrate. I don't want to make too big a deal out of it, but I wanted you to be there, as it was your clever idea.'

Hot tears prickled Darcy's eyes. 'Of course. I'd love that.' How she longed for him to say that he needed her. That he couldn't get through today without her by his side. She kissed him, her empathy ever-present. But also to stop herself from pushing for the impossible.

Now wasn't the time.

'Thank you...for asking me to share this with you and Rosie.' She stepped back from the warm, safe circle of his arms. 'I'll just get changed—help yourself to wine in the kitchen.'

Darcy raced upstairs and stripped off her interview clothes, choosing a comfy pair of jeans and her favourite snugly jumper. Ignoring why she needed its soft, fluffy comfort, she pressed her hand over her fluttering heart to steady her whirlwind thoughts. He'd come to her to share a massive emotional milestone. Could it mean that he'd opened his heart to the idea of more?

As she headed back down the stairs in her bare feet, the clatter of pots and pans making her stomach rumble, she tried to shove all doubts aside and just be there for Joe.

'Smells good,' she said, coming up beside him

and taking a grateful sip from the glass of red wine he handed her with one hand while jiggling the pan containing the sizzling steaks with the other.

Abandoning the cooking, he turned, scooped his arm around her waist, kissed her. She wanted to forget the demands of her unfed stomach and drag him upstairs now that they had the house to themselves. But tonight wasn't about her and her constant need for Joe. It was about him and Rosie, remembrance and celebration for a life cut too short.

Joe served the steaks onto two plates already laden with delicious salad and they carried plates and wine glasses to the table, where he'd even lit a bunch of candles Stella liked to burn.

So thoughtful. So romantic. So Joe…

'What reasons did they give for not offering you the job?' asked Joe, slicing into his perfectly medium steak.

Darcy shrugged, desperate to avoid voicing her biggest fears about him, but needing to know all the same. She wanted to trust him one hundred per cent. To give all of herself. More than that, she needed to know that he was on the same page as her when it came to them.

'Oh, the usual…' she said, her stomach now too unsettled to eat. 'Personality fit and experience.' She loaded her fork with salad anyway, ready to fill her mouth so she couldn't say anything to ruin tonight, but the words escaped anyway. 'A part of me was worried that perhaps you'd based my reference on our disastrous first meeting…'

Joe frowned, even though she'd punctuated her outrageous and unfounded accusation with a nervous giggle to soften its impact.

Darcy looked down at her plate and ploughed on, all her fears now rising to the surface as if she'd cut herself open. 'Or they could somehow tell from what you'd written that we're sleeping together… I know—silly.' She shook her head but the fear lingered, that rejection-sensitive part of her convinced that Joe's professional respect was a figment of her imagination. Waiting for his true colours to emerge, for him to condemn her surgical skills or, worse, to push her away.

She swallowed hard, her throat raw. She had to keep her feelings a secret. She couldn't tell him how much she cared about him, how she was falling in love with him. Not until she was sure that he was ready to accept her feelings.

Darcy pushed the food around her plate. She was already way more emotionally invested in Joe than he was in her. Part of her had hoped that he'd be overjoyed when she didn't get the job. That he'd admit they had something worth exploring beyond the handful of weeks she had left at City Hospital.

He shook his head and wiped his mouth with a napkin. 'Not that silly. I did struggle to stay professional when I wrote about you.'

Her heart surged, only to flop in the next heartbeat.

'Well, it's Manchester's loss. Let's hope that Thames Hospital—', which was not far from City Hospital '—or Newcastle see what an asset you'd be.'

Oh, how easily and with a sense of inevitability he compartmentalised what they'd shared.

Darcy nodded and swallowed her mouthful of salad, which tasted suspiciously like broken glass.

Darcy pushed the final birthday candle into the stack of pancakes and Joe lit it, his heart heavy as he tried to recall Rosie's incandescent smile. The only thing stopping him from breaking down completely was Darcy's encouraging, beautiful and genuine smile. Over the flickering candles, her eyes glowed with understanding and compassion so he almost lost himself in their depths.

With a heavy sigh, Joe finally admitted to himself why he'd come here tonight: he'd missed her, he needed her. She made him feel better, lighter, more like himself, his real self. His relief that she wouldn't be moving to Manchester was selfish and twisted, soured with the guilt that sliced between his ribs, because he had little to offer her in compensation.

She wasn't his therapy. He was responsible for his own emotional happiness, so he wanted—no, needed—to stop the panic that he could once again lose the only precious thing he had in his life. Before Darcy that emotional happiness hadn't mattered to him in the slightest. He'd been quite content to dwell with only his pain and his guilt.

But now…?

He couldn't shake the intrusive feelings that he could have more. Darcy was right. Joe's grief wouldn't bring Rosie back or keep her close. It wasn't his only connection to his little girl. There were so many other ways to honour and remember her, and she'd always live in his heart and soul.

'Will you sing with me?' His voice choked. Darcy squeezed his hand, her caring so humbling that all the things he wanted to say to her fled his mind.

'Yes, of course.'

They started singing 'Happy Birthday'. To his surprise Joe felt his smile come readily, naturally, his gaze flitting from the magical beauty of the ten tiny flames to the woman who'd given his life new purpose. Meaning. Hope.

He watched her watch him, emotions shifting inside him until he felt a wave of motion sickness. How would he get through the Christmas leukaemia fundraiser without her? Christmas Day, a day he dreaded, the anniversary of Rosie's death and her eleventh birthday…? Darcy was leaving, and he had no right to ask her to stay.

Being what she needed, a man who'd love her with everything he had, terrified Joe.

She had an exciting and fulfilled life ahead of her, but while she'd helped him realise that his future could be brighter, he had so far to go in order to be the man she deserved. He wouldn't hold her back on a false promise and he wouldn't let her down as her father had so many times.

The song ended. Joe blew out the candles and closed his eyes for a private second. 'Happy birthday, my darling,' he whispered, clinging to Darcy's hand tighter than ever, even while his mind rebelled at the idea he was growing too reliant on this woman.

He raised Darcy's hand to his mouth and pressed a kiss over her knuckles. 'Thanks for being there for me and for Rosie.'

'You're welcome, Joe,' she said, her eyes brimming with feelings it was hard for him to witness, because while he couldn't stay away, spending time with Darcy drew him closer and closer.

What if he unintentionally made her promises he wasn't sure he could keep?

'I need to go, actually,' he said, genuine regret tugging at his gut. 'I have to visit a private patient who's having a Hartmann's procedure the day after tomorrow.'

At her flash of disappointment, he tugged her into his arms and pressed his mouth to hers. 'Would you like to assist? I'd really appreciate the help.'

'Of course.' Darcy nodded, opened her mouth as if she wanted to say something and then closed it again.

He saw the yearning in her eyes. He wasn't stupid—he knew they'd diced with danger since Amsterdam. If Darcy felt even half of the emotional connection to him that he felt for her, she must wonder what their future might hold. He couldn't give her much in return for all the amazing gifts she'd given him, but he could at least be honest.

'You know,' he said, brushing his thumb across her soft bottom lip, 'I wish we'd met in another life, one where we were both open to finding love.' His stomach turned, but he pushed on. 'You are the whole package, Darcy. One day someone is going to love you and cherish you as you deserve. Maybe that someone is waiting in Newcastle.'

Joe swallowed the envy he had no right to feel.

'Maybe,' she said, her voice hollow. 'Come on.' She rose to her feet and reached for his hand to pull him up. 'You don't want to be late.'

No... And there were so many more things he wished he could make right as easily as showing up on time.

CHAPTER FOURTEEN

You have to tell him.

Stella's words ran through Darcy's mind from their late-night chat after Joe had left. Stella was a master at interrogation, and Darcy had blurted out her confession in a purgative rush. She was deeply in love with Joe. She'd never realistically be able to hide that from her sister for long. Stella knew Darcy wasn't the type to fall constantly in and out of love, so it was obvious to anyone with eyes.

Anyone except Joe.

Joe had been open and honest—the man to love and cherish Darcy, as he claimed she deserved, wasn't him. Why else would he suggest that she look for this mythical man in Newcastle? She hadn't even had her interview up north, but already he had her packed and delivered!

No wonder her emotions had got the better of her after he'd left.

They were equally fragile today, but there was

a glimmer of hope. Perhaps Stella was right. Perhaps Joe was determined not to stand in the way of her career. Perhaps his feelings matched hers, but he was too wrapped up in his fear to give them a voice. Perhaps if he knew how she felt about him, he might not relinquish her to a non-existent Geordie lover quite so readily.

Darcy breathed deeply against the nerves churning in her stomach. She dumped her scrubs in the linen bin near the door of the staff changing rooms and headed out to the foyer of the private hospital where she'd assisted Joe in the Hartmann's procedure. They'd spent the day operating together, both work-focused and avoiding any personal interaction. But the things she had to say bubbled up inside her, desperate to escape. They'd reached an impasse. She was moving on—the prestigious job at Thames Hospital, while her preferred position, wasn't guaranteed—and she didn't want to leave London, if she secured the Newcastle post, without him knowing her feelings.

She spotted Joe, a tall handsome figure near the exit, his head bent over his phone. Her pulse accelerated as it always did when he was close. Would she ruin their last few weeks together with her confession? Or would she earn what she wanted, working for it the way she'd always achieved?

Resolute, she crossed the foyer. Her feelings weren't the only thing they needed to discuss. This morning she'd calculated that her period was five days late. Intellectually, she knew it couldn't possibly mean she was pregnant—they'd used protection—but the niggle of doubt lodged in her brain all the same, and for a few minutes she allowed herself to wonder what if…

What if they could forge a future together, be a team in their private lives as well as at work? What if Darcy could finally put all of her fears aside and commit everything she had into making this relationship with Joe real and enduring? What if he could love her in return?

She saw the fantasy in her head and for the first time ever it seemed tangible and barely out of reach. Thrills of excitement danced along her nerve-endings as, side by side, they headed out to the car park.

When they were seated in Joe's car, driving back to City Hospital, Darcy could wait no longer. Perhaps their discussion around contraception would be the catalyst to a discussion of their future. Then she could tell him how she felt and perhaps that would be enough for him to realise he felt the same way.

Darcy dragged in a deep breath, actually tempted to cross her fingers for the first time since she was a kid. 'I um… I have something to tell you,' she said, choosing the easier of the two confessions to begin.

Joe raised his eyebrows in invitation, his focus on the traffic.

'It probably means nothing—' she brushed a speck of fluff from her trousers '—but I'm a few days late this month.' Darcy cleared her throat, which was gripped by nerves. 'I might just do a pregnancy test to stop myself worrying and waiting.'

Joe said nothing, sat frozen, staring straight ahead at the car in front.

Prickles of unease crept down Darcy's spine. The nerves flared and she prattled on, filling the loaded silence. 'I…thought you should know, but I'm sure it's no big deal…'

Of course, he'd be shocked initially, especially if he assumed she *was* pregnant, as she'd done for a split second that morning. But, of course, she wasn't. Any minute now they'd laugh about the absurdity of that likelihood, she'd pluck up the courage to tell him that she loved him and they'd move on to play the *what if?* game for their future.

Wordlessly, Joe pulled off the road and parked up in a side street lined by trees frosted with autumn colour.

The wait for him to speak seemed endless.

How had this taken such a serious turn so quickly? It wasn't going at all to plan.

Joe killed the engine and turned to face her. 'How late?' His tone was clipped, his mouth pinched in a small scowl. It reminded Darcy of the day they'd met, of his…disapproval and unfair judgement.

'Five or six days.' Her stomach griped, uneasy. He looked as if she'd punched him in the gut. 'But it's irrelevant. I can't be pregnant.'

His frown persisted as Darcy's indignation cracked open a sleepy eye.

'Are you normally regular?' he asked in his surgeon's voice, as if taking a medical history from a poorly compliant patient. Darcy felt like a naughty little girl.

'Yes… But I figured it was the stress of job hunting.' She had the Thames interview tomorrow. 'Perhaps we should have had a discussion around the consequences before we started sleeping together.' She pointed out the obvious now that she knew his opinion, which was etched on his face.

His expression, the frustration in his eyes, bordered on horrified. Darcy shivered, chilled to the bone by his cold reaction. Did he not want children full stop, or just not now? Perhaps he didn't want them with *her*.

She just about stopped her hand from covering her mouth.

'We used condoms,' he said, matter of fact. 'I know they're not foolproof, but you can't be pregnant.' It sounded as if he was forbidding it rather than rationalising the probability.

Darcy closed her eyes as nausea threatened. He'd offered no reassurance, no consideration of how she might be concerned, no promise that whatever happened—positive or negative—they'd work out the consequences together, as a team.

Because he didn't see them as a team outside of the hospital. He didn't have feelings for her.

'I agree. It's highly unlikely.' Darcy swallowed the irrational tears clogging her throat. Deep down she knew the possibility that she might be pregnant could be a trigger for Joe, but a part of her had hoped their discussion would turn to their future or the growing seriousness of what had started as a fling between colleagues but was now more.

Except in Joe's eyes it wasn't. That seriousness was one-sided, representative of *her* feelings, not his.

How could she have been so stupid and so blind?

Joe's emotions were still locked away, safe and secure and unchanged from the first day they'd met, despite all they'd shared. He couldn't have any feelings for her, otherwise they'd be able to talk about this, laugh together, figure out a plan, as she'd fantasised.

But fantasies were pointless. Hadn't she learned that by now?

The slap of rejection landed like a blow. Darcy snatched her gaze away from the sickening view of Joe's conflicted expression and stared blindly out of the car window. What had she done? She'd fallen for a man who was aeons behind, emotionally. She was about to confess that she loved him, that she'd embraced the belief that she could finally have it all, the career she loved and a happy personal life. That she could at last be enough, be everything to someone.

How had she fallen for the wrong man again? This time one who could never love her back because somehow he believed that opening his heart to her meant betraying the memory of his daughter.

Joe gunned the engine. 'We'll get a test right now,' he said, all businesslike and assertive, the way he behaved in Theatre. 'There's a chemist down the road.'

He'd slipped so effortlessly into control mode, the perfectionism he used as a shield, that she almost agreed to his irrelevant and invasive suggestion. But she wasn't a patient, or something to be managed, fixed and filed. An inconvenience.

'Stop. I'm not a problem you can fix with your usual thorough approach.' The low volume of her request impressed Darcy. Outwardly she must appear calm, but inside she boiled and bubbled like molten lava.

'This isn't about an unplanned pregnancy,' she said, humiliated that he couldn't see the problem here for himself. Devastated that she'd misjudged him so spectacularly.

Joe stared, a confused furrow between his brows. 'Of course it is…'

Fingers of dread gripped Darcy's throat. She had two choices. One, take Joe's urgent pregnancy test, fake jovial relief when it was negative and forget about confessing her feelings—they were clearly horribly unrequited anyway. Or two, put Joe on the spot instead and demand that they have the second conversation about his feelings for her.

'What else is it about?' Joe rubbed a hand over his face, clearly confused and perhaps a little impatient.

She understood that he'd be keen to have this matter nicely rectified so he could shuffle back into his emotional hermit hideaway.

Looking into his eyes, which showed only fear, a piece of Darcy shattered like the handle snapping off a fine bone china teacup. For self-preservation she should back down, pretend that all she wanted from him was a cordial end to their fling, along with his glowing professional reference, and move on, forgetting that she'd opened herself up to a world of pain by falling in love with her unreachable boss.

Except Stella was right—if you didn't try you couldn't be rejected, but nor could you be accepted. Joe had shown her that she was good enough, despite her past. He believed in her and if she could reach the pinnacle of a stressful and demanding career she could do anything, including being brave and honest, even if he might not be ready to hear it. She needed to lay everything on the line, for herself, to prove that she'd been all in, before he…freaked out.

Now was the time for the biggest push of her life.

'It's about us, Joe,' she said, her vision blurring with the effort of staring at his handsome face and panicked eyes. 'About the chasm between us emotionally.'

Joe's frown deepened as if he genuinely had no clue that her feelings might be involved. He looked so aghast that a wave of empathy might have swiped her feet from under her if she hadn't already been seated.

Darcy hardened her resolve, prepared to hammer the last nail in the coffin of their relationship. If he couldn't see a future with her and a life they might create together, he'd definitely be unprepared to hear what she was about to say next.

'I love you.' The words flew free at last, but minus the expected wave of euphoria she'd imagined. 'I've been desperately trying to hold that inside because I knew you might not be ready to hear it.'

She couldn't switch off her empathy for him. That he could offer her nothing in the way of commitment was due to him clinging to the fear that he'd somehow love Rosie less if he allowed himself to be happy.

'I thought when you shared Rosie's birthday with me,' she continued, 'that you might be moving in the right direction, that you might trust me and want more from me, but you don't. Your face tells me exactly what you're feeling—terrified and about to retreat.'

He winced, looking down at his lap. 'Darcy, I—'

'It's okay.' She couldn't hear his excuses and platitudes—they'd destroy what was left of her composure. He'd never promised her love and for ever. He'd promised her nothing. 'I should have known better than to trust my instincts. They've always landed me here—hurt and alone.'

She needed to escape. To get away from his sympathetic stare.

'You're not alone,' he said. 'You're pushing this too far… I—'

'Oh, don't worry, Joe,' Darcy interrupted. 'I know you're an honourable man who would support me and our non-existent child, but I don't need that from you.' Darcy sucked in a breath laced with her last shred of courage. 'I needed a sign that we were on the same path, that this relationship was going somewhere. And now I have my sign. You're not ready to feel anything for me and the worst part is that… I understand.' A film of tears blurred her vision. 'I'm not even angry. I'm just empty.'

Yet again she'd chosen a man who didn't see the real Darcy, didn't *want* the real Darcy. The reality of any future they might share was one of Darcy making all of the sacrifices, never quite sure if she was good enough, and Joe lagging behind emotionally, scared to commit in case it changed the status quo he'd built around his wounded heart.

Darcy reached for her bag from the passenger side footwell and pulled at the lock on the car door.

'Wait—you can't just leave. We need to talk about this.' Joe shook his head as if trying to clear the fog from his brain. He seemed dazed, as if the idea of feeling something for her was so alien to him he couldn't quite grasp the concept. 'I'm not saying the right things…' But where he might be uncertain, Darcy now saw everything clearly.

Her heart clenched in one final spasm as she traced his features with her blurry stare. She swallowed, hardened her faltering heart, ignoring the pain that had nothing to do with the anatomical muscular pump in her chest and everything to do with her foolishness.

Of course he'd rejected her. Hadn't a part of her always expected it?

'Words are overrated, Joe. Promises are broken every day. I'll get over this, don't worry.' She'd got over her father's trail of dismissal and indifference and she'd got over failing Dean's expectations. 'I'm just embarrassed that I was stupid enough to believe my own hype when I know differently.'

Before she could bare her soul further, she fled, jogging towards the main road and jumping aboard the first bus that stopped. She had no idea where it was going, just as she had no plan for how she'd face him tomorrow. All she knew was that her tomorrows wouldn't include Joe.

CHAPTER FIFTEEN

JOE STARED AT the computer screen, hollow-eyed and hollow-chested from reading the contents of his latest email from Darcy. She'd secured the consultant position at Thames Hospital and handed in her notice. Taking her fortnight of unused annual leave into account meant she'd only be with him at City for another three weeks.

Then she'd be out of his life for ever, just the way she must believe he wanted.

Joe scrubbed a hand over his face, frustration a tight knot in his stomach. She'd told him that she loved him and he'd said nothing. He must have acted as if falling in love again was the worst thing that could happen to him; the fear of exactly that had certainly ground all his mental faculties to a halt. He'd been in shock, yes, and she hadn't given him the chance to explain his thoughts and feelings after her double whammy bombshell she'd delivered in his car. She'd pushed him away and pushed onwards regardless, the way she'd always done. To prove that she was okay without him?

That should bring him relief. He had no doubt that she would be fine. But he couldn't claim the same.

Joe felt as if he'd been hit by a truck and he only had himself to blame.

He and Darcy had come full circle. She warily avoided him in the hospital and he'd focused on his busy week in order to ignore the fact that he was floundering around for a way to make it right.

All he could think about was his future and how it compared to the images that had flashed briefly and brilliantly before him when Darcy had told him that she loved him.

Sick to his stomach, he pulled out his phone and opened her last text message, which had been sent the night everything around them had collapsed.

Pregnancy test negative.

Three little words. Three enormous words, because they forced him to truly search his heart in a way he hadn't done for years. They forced his past and his future to collide, forced him to acknowledge what was becoming increasingly unthinkable.

Life without Darcy.

His throat closed in panic; he couldn't allow her to leave this way.

A knock at the door prevented further futile self-reflection. Laura entered, carrying a small bag.

'Is it that time already?' Joe asked, rising from his desk to meet her halfway across the room. He pressed a kiss to her cheek in greeting and glanced down at her baby bump. 'How was your appointment? Is he growing and healthy? The right number of digits?' She'd been at City Hospital this morning for an obstetric appointment and ultrasound scan.

'Yes, all perfectly normal.' Laura smiled, kneading the small of her back with her free hand. 'I brought the things you asked for.' She held the bag aloft, her eyes clouded with understanding.

Joe stared at the bag as if it contained the secrets of the universe—wonderful but terrifying. Then he breathed through his gut reaction and took the offering, peeking inside.

'Thanks for this; I appreciate it.' Joe placed the bag carefully on his desk as if it held fragile birds' eggs. 'Do you want a seat? A glass of water?'

Laura settled into the sofa with the protracted sigh of a heavily pregnant woman. 'Yes, please.'

Joe collected a glass of water, eyeing the bag of Rosie's things with longing. He'd examine the contents later. At home. Alone. So that he could fully immerse himself in the memories the items would surely evoke. Happy memories. Treasured memories.

At Darcy's suggestion he'd asked Laura to select some keepsakes from Rosie's room at the house that he could hold onto. It was time he stopped punishing himself and started honouring Rosie in a way that would make her proud.

If only he could fix what he'd allowed to happen with Darcy so easily, not that he was a fully recovered grief addict, but he wanted to find balance. To be a better version of himself. To be worthy of the wonderful woman who'd shown him another way forward. Darcy.

He and Laura chatted for a few minutes about due dates and baby names, the nostalgia heavy in the air. But neither was it as overwhelming as it had once been. That was down to Darcy. She'd showed him a path through the trees that he couldn't see alone. She'd led him to that first clearing in the woods when she'd awoken him to emotions, negative and positive and so human he was ashamed to acknowledge he hadn't found the way unaided. But they'd been a team. He was man enough to accept he wasn't an island, that he needed people.

Really, he just needed Darcy.

'That's the third sigh in as many minutes,' said Laura. 'Why don't you ask me for advice so I can waddle off home and put up my swollen feet?'

Joe sighed again, this one deep enough to operate all of the hospital's ventilators. He looked at his ex-wife, marvelled not for the first time at the contentment glowing in her features, at the hope shining in her eyes.

'How did you do it?' he asked. 'How did you move on without feeling as if you were losing more of her?'

Laura stared at her lap, the flash of pain moving across her face telling Joe that their daughter was never far from her mind either, in spite of appearances. It buoyed his spirits. Laura had found a way to live with her grief and allow herself to be happy.

'I love Rosie as much as the day she was born.' She put her hand on her belly, over her second child. 'Perhaps even more.'

'Me, too,' agreed Joe, sorry that he'd brought sadness into the room, but needing to be a man who could face his demons and be what Darcy deserved.

If only he could grasp that elusive thread, that lifeline Laura seemed to have caught hold of. Was it just as Darcy said—choosing to live with the memories in a different way?

'I didn't want to be alone for ever,' she said. 'I wanted to smile again, laugh again, find other joys. The small things, you know?'

Joe nodded, a secret smile tugging at his mouth as he recalled flickering candles atop a stack of pancakes and the way they'd reflected in Darcy's beautiful eyes.

'Remember her infectious giggle?' Laura smiled at him through the sheen of tears. 'One of us would crack up, and then she'd start, and then we'd laugh harder because her laughter was such a delightful sound we never wanted her to stop.'

Joe nodded, his chest in a vice as he held onto the image, the memories.

'Somehow,' continued Laura, 'I just knew that Rosie, our wonderful girl, would want me to be happy. That she's watching me and when I laugh she laughs. She can't help herself.' Laura blinked rapidly, clearing the moisture from her eyes. 'I want her to laugh, Joe, every day. Wherever she is, I need to know that she's giggling.'

Joe nodded, his grin wide and spontaneous at the image Laura created. 'That's perfect. I want that, too.'

She nodded and rose to her feet. 'Good, that's the easy part. The hard part is finding out what makes you happy and doing that every day.' She cast him a speculative look, feminine wisdom etched into her insightful smile.

'I think I might know what that is.' Joe's heart hammered. He needed to talk to Darcy.

'Good.' Laura squeezed his arm as she skirted him on her way to the door. 'And another piece of advice, which I kind of shouldn't need to tell you, but will hopefully steer you in the right direction in the future.' She turned in the doorway and pointed at his chest. 'Never make a pregnant woman cry.'

Joe grinned. 'Thanks. I'll remember that.'

Hiding away in the office beside the on-call room, Darcy pulled up the erect chest X-ray of the seventy-year-old woman she'd just admitted, noting the two crescents of black under the diaphragm denoting escaped air. She made a note in the patient file and ordered a host of blood tests on the computer. Then she texted the foundation doctor with instructions to start working up the patient for Theatre. Mrs Hancock would need a laparotomy. Perhaps she'd invite the foundation doctor to scrub in and assist. She had no idea where Joe was, despite them being on call tonight.

Perhaps he was avoiding her, the way she'd been keeping too busy to bump into him…

Darcy pressed her hand to her breastbone, breathed through the tightness which had settled there the minute she'd walked away from

Joe's car and jumped on that number ten bus. Yes, her professional confidence was at an all-time high. Under Joe's tutelage these past months she'd flourished, become even more autonomous. A good thing, as she was about to become a consultant, in charge of her own team of junior doctors and ultimately responsible for the patients under her care.

But personally… There she seemed to be travelling backwards. Still making errors of judgement, still choosing the wrong man. Still scared to fully commit and push for what she truly wanted. What she deserved: love.

The door swung open and in strode Joe. His eyes lit up with relief, and Darcy had to look away to stop herself flying into his arms, divesting him of his scrubs and forcing him to love her in return. Because, no matter how deeply she'd retreated into her protective shell at the first hint of his rejection, if anything she felt worse, not better.

So fight for him. Push.

Only it was easier to focus on the here and now rather than dissect the mess that was them. Did she have it in her to commit to the added responsibilities of a new job and to struggle over her feelings for Joe? They were so emotionally distant she might as well be going to Newcastle.

Walking away, no matter how much it hurt, would save her heartache in the long run. Wouldn't it?

'I've just admitted a seventy-year-old woman with abdominal pain and pneumoperitoneum,' she said, her tone businesslike, reminding her of that first day when she'd shoved her diagnostic skills under his nose for Mr Clarke and his appendix. 'Her blood work is underway. She has no pre-existing medical conditions apart from well-controlled hypertension. I'd like to add her to tonight's op list for an exploratory laparotomy.'

Surely she must have imagined the flicker of amused indulgence in Joe's eyes as he stared back. 'Since when did you need my permission?'

Darcy shot him what she hoped was a look that reflected her incredulity. 'Since we started going backwards—you disapproving of my every move and double-checking my work was how we began, after all.'

Darcy turned back to the computer and logged off. It hurt to look at him, knowing that he'd never be hers. She sensed Joe move closer and her hand faltered on the mouse.

'We're not moving backwards, Darcy—only forwards. Together.'

Darcy snorted, shoved down the flare of hope that warmed her blood and rose to her feet. 'I don't think so.' She turned to face him, forced herself to meet his deep brown eyes. ‘I’m moving to Thames and I truly wish you well, Joe.’ Her voice almost cracked because she’d never meant anything more. She loved him and she wanted his pain to lessen, to end, even if she wouldn’t be around to witness his ongoing journey of healing.

Sometimes people were too broken to be there for others, and Darcy deserved a man who loved her with everything he had.

She looked down, away from his searching stare, which left her raw and exposed. ‘Excuse me.’ She stepped sideways to bypass his solid presence blocking her escape.

‘Oh, no.’ He reached for her arm, his touch everything she wanted. ‘No more running and no more pushing me away.’

Darcy levelled her least tolerant glare on him while her heart raced way too fast for safety. ‘I’m too tired for this, Joe.’

Heartsick more like.

Because he was right; she had pushed him that day she’d told him that she loved him. As much as she’d expected his rejection, known deep down that Joe was still working on some major personal stuff, she couldn’t bear to hear her worst fears vocalised. That he could never love her back. That she wasn’t enough. That he didn’t want her.

Joe tilted her chin up until their eyes met once

more. Her heart leapt, pulsing to her extremities. Being this close to him, a step away from everything she wanted, was torture.

How would she survive the next few hours, let alone the next three weeks?

'Too tired to love me?' he asked, pushing that stubborn lock of hair back from her cheek. 'Or too tired to hear how I love you, too?'

Darcy's heart stopped for a beat, a second, a third, stuttering back to life with her short gasp. He'd never be so cruel as to toy with her emotions, and yet he couldn't mean it…

Joe ignored her shocked expression and ploughed on. 'I never got to have my say that day when you thought you might be pregnant.'

Hadn't he received her text, telling him of the negative test? Was he simply saying all of this out of some sense of twisted loyalty?

She couldn't process his words. She couldn't organise her own thoughts.

'Well, I'm not pregnant—' she stepped aside, away from the wall of his body '—so this conversation doesn't need to happen.'

He stepped in front of her once more, gripped her upper arms, forced her eyes back to his. 'If you'd given me a chance to organise my thoughts that day and disentangle them from my emotions, you might have learned that I felt a thousand things during that conversation and only one of them was fear.'

Darcy nodded, only hearing him admit to being too scared to give them a chance.

'I *was* scared,' he confirmed. 'I still am. I never thought I'd have another chance at love, at happiness. For a long time, I felt unworthy of a second shot. But I realised that my fear was a symptom that I'd already fallen in love. With you.'

'Joe…' She couldn't bear to hear any more; her battered heart was too fragile.

He swallowed and she saw his turmoil swirling in his eyes. 'I'm not going to sugar-coat it, Darcy. The idea of being a father again terrifies me.'

'I understand.' Her heart cracked a little more. She'd always imagined that one day she'd have children, but right now she loved Joe enough to promise never to put him through that fear.

'But you ran,' he said. 'You did what you've done since the day I met you: push. You pushed me away. I understand why, and I ache here—' he pressed his hand over his sternum '—for the rejection you've been through. But just like I need to work on my grief, learn to express it in healthier ways, you need to work on your knee-jerk reaction to anything you perceive as rejection.'

She nodded, her eyes stinging, because they were no further forward. He was right, his conclusion one she'd come to herself in the past few days when she'd thought they were over and she'd been forced to self-reflect. She *had* pushed him away at the first hint of negative reaction. She'd pushed before she could be pushed.

It didn't lessen the pain though.

'Thanks for the analysis. I'll be sure to take your comments on board next time I get involved with the wrong man.' No, she didn't mean that. 'I'm sorry, you're right. I have pushed people away first.'

But with Joe she'd been finally ready to let go fully and risk it all.

'There won't be a next time, Darcy.' He stepped closer, his hand sliding down her arm to grip her hand. 'I regret my slow reaction when you told me you loved me. But we're stuck with each other.' His smile all but broke her in two. 'We love each other and we're going to work this and any other snag out during our relationship.'

'You want a relationship…?' Blood whooshed through her ears.

'Of course.' He smiled and her eyes drank in the beautiful sight. 'Did you miss the part where I told you I love you?'

She nodded, her eyes filling with moisture.

He raised her hand to his mouth and kissed her knuckles slowly, one swipe, two, tender and reverent.

'Joe, I want a relationship, too. I promise we can take it as slow as you need.'

He shook his head, his self-assured grin telling her everything would be fine as long as they were together. 'I don't want slow. I want you as you are.' He brushed his lips over hers. 'Humans aren't perfect,' he said, his eyes brimming with a million emotions. 'We make mistakes. We say the wrong things. We feel too much sometimes, and it makes us a little bit crazy. But I've been married before, so I'm the one with the experience here. You're going to have to trust me on this one. A marriage, lifelong commitment, takes work and just wait until our family comes along. That will test us in ways we never even considered. You'll probably constantly push your agenda and I'll likely consider every possible consequence in minute detail, but we'll always get there in the end.'

Was he saying he wanted for ever with her? Marriage? Children?

Could she do this? Take the leap, put in the work and last the distance, despite the bumps in the road that might make her nervous? Yes! She was Darcy Wright. She could do anything she set her mind to, including loving Joe without reservation, wholly and fully vulnerable.

He cupped her face, holding her eye contact. 'I know you're scared,' he said, breathing against her lips. 'I am, too. But I'm more terrified of the pain of losing you than I am of risking my heart again. So I need you to trust me. To put your hand in mine and come with me on this journey. I need you, your strength and your determination and instincts. I need you on my team.'

Darcy nodded, too choked to speak.

'You make me happy, Darcy, and I want to be happy every day for the rest of my life. I'm ready.'

Just like the first time they'd kissed, which was full of frustration and pent-up emotion, Darcy flew at Joe, slamming her mouth over his to shut him up. His *I love you, too*, rang in her ears. In her yearning and disbelief she'd missed at least half of his spiel, but she understood the gist.

She could have everything she wanted and she was ready too, to hold on tight and never let go.

Joe banded his arms around her back and hoisted her feet from the floor, stumbling the few paces into the on-call room. He slammed the door closed and pressed her back up against it, jamming his leg between hers and tangling his hands in her hair so he could kiss her back. Darcy never wanted this moment to end, except reality beckoned…

'Joe…' she said, a million explosions detonating in her nervous system, which struggled to process so much happiness. 'I need to go and fix Mrs Hancock…'

He nodded and took her hand, his confident smile filling her with hope and certainty that working together, being together, loving each other, they could achieve anything.

'First we fix Mrs Hancock, then we focus on us.' He raised her hand to his mouth and kissed it, his eyes promising everything she'd ever wanted.

'Deal,' Darcy agreed.

EPILOGUE

Three months later

A MILLION TWINKLING lights sparkled overhead, cloaking the ceiling in festive magic. Darcy blinked, glancing over at Joe. She already had enough stars in her eyes just looking at her man.

Joe filled a tuxedo like no other man on earth, almost as good as he looked in his scrubs. Her mouth dried as she performed a quick calculation of the time remaining before she could drag him home and worship every inch of him. There weren't enough hours in the day…

Joe finished his brief conversations with the chair of the Leukaemia Foundation and slipped his arm around her waist, directing her to the terrace, where a million more lights twinkled overhead.

'It's freezing. Where are we going?' she said, surprised that she was getting Joe to herself earlier than expected.

Joe shrugged off his jacket and draped it over Darcy's shoulders, the warmth seeping into her skin and his scent filling her head. 'I want to get you alone. We haven't had two minutes to ourselves tonight.'

'Well, you're the host,' she reminded him. 'This fundraiser wouldn't have happened without you. You're a man in demand.' Since he'd joined the board of the Leukaemia Foundation charity he'd found renewed purpose. He still operated four days a week at City, but that he'd begun something for himself, a job that refilled the tanks, told Darcy just how far he'd come.

Joe pulled her into his arms and settled his mouth over hers in a long, slow and thorough kiss that left Darcy weak-kneed.

'What was that for?' she said, gripping his biceps.

His eyes shone with his feelings, so open and vulnerable she was humbled by his courage. 'I love you.'

'I love you, too,' she whispered, her head spinning at how lucky she was to have found Joe.

'I missed waking up with you this morning.' He nuzzled her neck, his lips soft and his stubble tickling a path of delight to all of her erogenous zones.

Darcy closed her eyes and dropped her head back, giving him access. 'I had to go into Thames early. I had a new registrar to welcome.' Only now work was the last thing on her mind.

'Did you go easy on them?' To Darcy's dismay, he stopped the path of kisses, wrapped his arms around her and began to shuffle his feet, swirling her around in a slow dance under the lights and the stars.

Darcy smiled up at Joe. 'I took your advice and told him that I liked things done a certain way and he'd just have to get used to it.'

Joe grinned with approval. 'Is he any good? Because a competent registrar is worth their weight in gold, in my experience.'

Darcy rolled her eyes, her mind anywhere but at the hospital now that his hands were caressing her bare back underneath his jacket. 'I don't know yet… It's early days.'

Joe held her close and lowered his mouth to her ear so she shuddered. 'But the best registrars show you what they are made of from day one.'

She laughed again and Joe took the opportunity to plunder her neck, laying down a trail of kisses in her most sensitive spots.

'Well, train him up quickly,' he said as he reached her exposed collarbone.

'I will…' Darcy's mind grew foggy as arousal dragged her away from the topic of conversation. 'Why do you care? Can't we stop all this chit-chat and just go home?'

Joe pressed his hand into the small of her back and crushed her to his chest. 'He'll need to be proficient enough to hold the fort while you're away.'

Away…? Perhaps she was too aroused to keep track of the thread of the conversation. Had she missed something?

'Where am I going?'

Joe smiled, reaching into his pocket. 'On our honeymoon.'

He stepped back, dropped to one knee and opened the ring box. 'Darcy, you've given me so much, and all I have to give you in return is me. Will you be on my team for ever? Will you marry me?'

Darcy gasped, blind to the beauty of the diamond, seeing only the dazzling love shining in Joe's eyes.

'Yes,' she said, her voice wobbly with tears. 'Will you be on my team, too?' she asked, dragging him to his feet.

'Always.' And then he kissed her.

* * * * *

If you enjoyed this story, check out these other great reads from JC Harroway

Tempting the Enemy
Bound to You
Bad Mistake
Bad Reputation

All available now!